'I'll say this for you, you do have a certain dry wit that I haven't found in too many members of the opposite sex.'

'Maybe you've been hanging around with the wrong members of the opposite sex,' Emma said, trying to stifle the spurt of pleasure his compliment had given her.

'Maybe I have. Would you say it's too late to remedy that?' His voice was low and warm. Suddenly the room felt hot, too hot for comfort, and tiny needles were pricking her skin.

'Far too late,' she replied crisply. Perhaps she was imagining the speculative intimacy behind his words, or maybe he was playing some kind of game. Whatever, she would do well to remember that she could not afford to let her guard drop. Not for an instant.

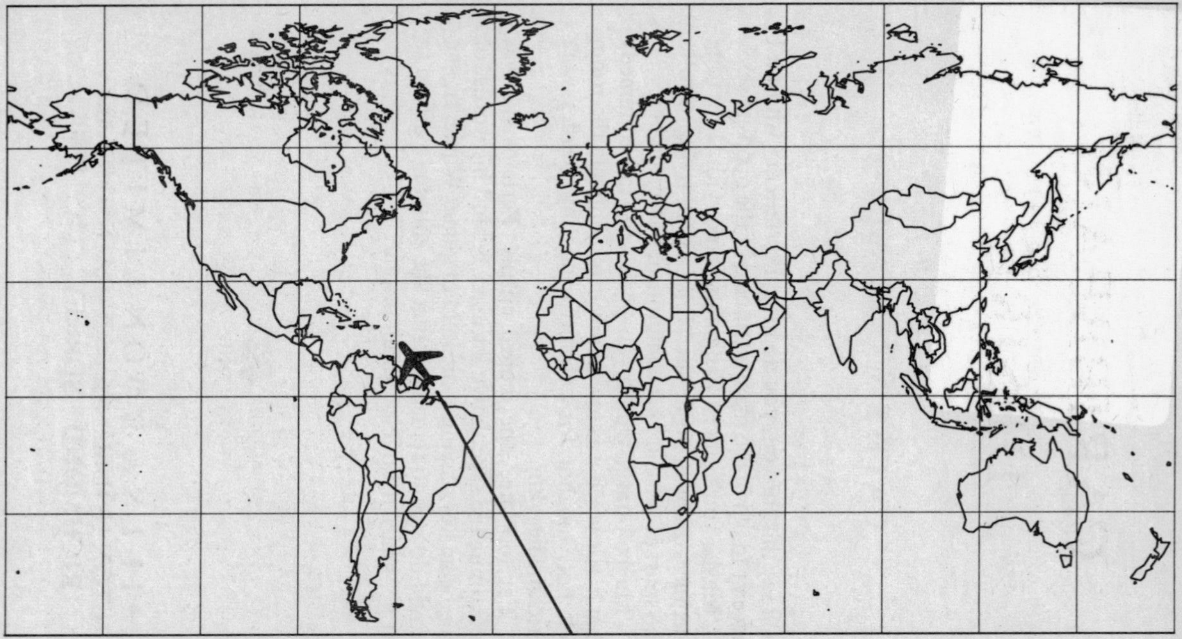

TOBAGO

CARIBBEAN DESIRE

BY

CATHY WILLIAMS

MILLS & BOON LIMITED
ETON HOUSE 18-24 PARADISE ROAD
RICHMOND SURREY TW9 1SR

First published in Great Britain 1991
by Mills & Boon Limited

This edition 1991

ISBN 0 263 77239 X

Set in Times Roman 10 on 11 pt.
01-9109-56183 C

Made and printed in Great Britain

CHAPTER ONE

EMMA had no idea who to look out for, and she didn't much care. She was at last at the tiny Tobago airport, only a few miles away from her destination, and that fluttering, panicky feeling of wondering whether she had done the right thing was back with her again.

This time, though, it was too late to do anything about it.

She collected her suitcases from the carousel, glancing interestedly around her, and then went to wait outside for her ride to the Jackson villa.

Even if the trip was a complete fiasco, she thought logically, at least it would give her the opportunity to sample something of the West Indies. How many of her friends would give their eye-teeth to be where she was now?

She looked around at the bustle of dark bodies standing in groups chatting, selling local fruit to the tourists, at the blindingly clear blue skies, at the Technicolor green of all the foliage. It was all a world apart from the grey, dismal skies of England which she had left behind.

She glanced across to the row of brightly dressed, ebony-skinned women standing behind their stalls of local sweets, lethargically fanning themselves with folded newspapers, and thought that it wasn't merely the scenery which provided such a contrast. Even the pace of life seemed slower, as though the warm, sweet breeze made people more easy-going, less in a frenetic rush to get somewhere.

Little snatches of their sing-song conversation reached her ears, and Emma made an effort to relax, to ignore that cramped, nervous feeling in the pit of her stomach which threatened to overwhelm her completely.

She had spent the last ten months weighing up the pros and cons of this trip, for heaven's sake; surely she should be feeling a little more confident about the whole thing?

It would help, of course, if the car would only come to collect her. If nothing else, it would give her less time to sit around feeling tense and queasy.

When all the flight arrangements had been made, she had been told that Alistair's gardener and houseboy would be there to meet her at the airport. Maybe, she thought hopefully, he was there and looking for her, although that didn't seem possible. It was hardly as though she blended into the background. With her long corn-blonde plait and pale complexion she stuck out like a sore thumb.

She dumped her suitcases on the ground and perched precariously on one of them, her slim arms clasped around her knees. All the doubts and indecisions that had plagued her ever since her decision to come to Tobago resurfaced with alarming force, and at the bottom of them all was the inevitable question: would it have been better to leave the past alone?

She was so absorbed in her thoughts that she was totally unaware of approaching footsteps.

'You must be Emma Belle. I'm here to meet you.' The man's voice was deep, with a lazy drawl and the merest hint of an English accent.

Emma looked up with a start and was struck by a fleeting impression of height and power. She clambered to her feet, feeling hot and distracted under his scrutiny, and inwardly thinking that the least he could do was offer to help her up instead of keeping his hands thrust firmly in his trouser pockets. She bent to retrieve her suitcase, and a tanned arm shot out, taking it from her.

'Allow me.'

'I can handle it myself,' Emma said, feeling peculiarly defensive.

'Fine.' Without another word, the man turned his back and began striding towards the car park, with Emma doing her best to keep pace with him.

'Could you slow down?' she panted in frustration. 'I happen to be lumbered with two suitcases and two holdalls. You can hardly expect me to keep pace with you!'

The man stopped abruptly and turned towards her. 'You did say you could manage,' he said mildly. Emma looked up at him, taking in the hard planes of his face, the thick black hair, the vivid blue eyes which were staring at her with what seemed like more than a bit of superiority.

She flushed, immediately annoyed that someone whom she had met less than ten minutes ago was managing quite successfully to get underneath her normally calm, unshakeable exterior. Of course, she thought, he had caught her at a vulnerable time. She was tired, nervous and hot. Still, she was unused to being ruffled by members of the opposite sex, especially one whose sexuality was so blatantly obvious.

He was still staring at her, and she looked away hurriedly.

'Are you Alistair Jackson's gardener?' she asked suspiciously, thinking that she had never seen a gardener who looked as arrogant as this one before.

'No.'

'Who are you, then?' He could be anybody, she thought. There was a latent aggression to him that she didn't like one bit. And it didn't just stop at his physique, either. The man was either in a very bad mood, or else he was simply threatening by nature. Whatever,

Emma decided that she wasn't going another step further until he explained himself.

She dropped her suitcases and folded her arms.

'Well?' she demanded. 'Who are you? I was told that I would be met here by Mr Jackson's gardener. I have no intention of going a step further until you tell me who you are and show me some sort of proof that you're authorised to collect me.'

'Proof? Authorised?' The man gave a short laugh, his blue eyes sweeping scornfully over her. 'You either follow me, or else you spend the rest of the day sweltering here in the sun.' He snatched her suitcases up as though they weighed nothing, and resumed his walking.

Emma hurried along behind him. She was not accustomed to being treated like this. Over the years she had cultivated a cool, aloof veneer that commanded respect. She liked being in control.

'You could at least tell me your name!' she panted furiously, noticing out of the corner of her eye that a few of the nearby locals were watching them, obviously amused.

This made her even more annoyed. Just who did he think he was? God knew what a fool she must look, stumbling behind this tall, raven-haired *barbarian*, her hair unravelling from its carefully woven plait, her fine features distorted with anger.

Not that he seemed to give a damn what sort of impression he was making on the people around them. He continued to stride purposefully away from the airport, obviously confident that she had no choice but to run behind him, making a complete spectacle of herself into the bargain.

'Your name?' she yelled furiously.

'Sorry,' the man said without turning around, and without sounding in the slightest bit apologetic, 'didn't I mention it?'

'No, you didn't!'

'I'm Conrad DeVere.' He stopped abruptly in front of a shiny but old Land Rover and began unlocking the boot.

Emma stared at him. Of course! She should have recognised him! In fact, she would have recognised him if the damned man hadn't been so rude and unforthcoming. He could have been King Kong and she probably wouldn't have known it.

The grainy grey newspaper print did nothing for him, she acknowledged reluctantly. He was not a man to be casually overlooked. She looked at him covertly as he slung her cases into the car boot.

Whizz kid in the financial world, heart-throb with women—just the sort of arrogant type she disliked. His attitude towards her only confirmed it. Any social graces the man had, he obviously wasn't wasting on her. Emma climbed into the passenger seat of the car and strapped herself in.

'I've heard of you,' she said, looking at his hard profile, the strong, tanned hands on the steering-wheel.

'No doubt you have,' Conrad replied drily. 'And what have you heard from my loyal band of tabloid reporters?'

She chose to ignore the lazy sarcasm in his voice.

'You handle all of Alistair Jackson's business interests, don't you? In addition to your own?' In fact, Conrad DeVere's interests were as extensive as Alistair's. Maybe even more so. He seemed to own everything, from hotels across Europe and America to property development companies; even, if she remembered correctly, several chemical plants.

His face appeared in the newspapers with nauseating regularity. She looked at that face now and decided that she didn't like it. Too sexy. Too confident. Too assured. The sort of face that belonged to a man who didn't really give a damn whose toes he trod on.

'Been doing your homework?' He switched on the engine, and began to manoeuvre the car out of the car park.

Something in his tone of voice made Emma's hackles rise.

'It's not exactly a trade secret,' she snapped. 'Besides, it's part of my job to find out as much as I can about the people I work with. It makes it easier to know what they're talking about when we begin working. Anyway,' she said coldly, 'what are you doing over here? Aren't Mr Jackson's head offices in America and London? Not to mention yours?'

She glanced out of the window at the picture-postcard scenery flashing past, glimpses of bright blue sea in strips against the horizon, whole tracts of land covered with tall, gently swaying coconut trees. It would have been much more enjoyable if she weren't stuck in a car next to someone to whom she had taken an instant dislike.

She didn't like his attitude, she didn't like his lack of politeness, and she certainly didn't like the way he had managed to shake her.

'I'm here because of you,' he said, taking his eyes off the road for an instant to glance at her.

'Me? Why?'

'I've wanted to meet you, to see what you're like.' His voice implied that he didn't particularly like what he saw, and Emma's mouth tightened.

'How flattering,' she said sarcastically. 'I didn't realise, when I accepted this job to help Alistair Jackson with his biography, that I would be privileged to the once-over by the great Conrad DeVere.'

His face hardened and Emma felt a quiver of alarm shoot through her. There was definitely something threatening about this man, but if he thought that he could intimidate her, for whatever reason, then he was in for a big surprise.

'I wanted to see for myself who would be working with Alistair. I hardly expected someone young and attractive.'

'Meaning?' Something about his tone of voice was making her uneasy.

'Meaning that I find it slightly surprising that a girl like you is willing to confine herself to life on a remote island, merely for the altruistic delights of working with an old man.'

'I don't know what you're getting at,' Emma said frigidly, knowing precisely what he was getting at and not liking it one bit.

'Oh, don't pretend you don't know what I'm talking about.'

'I'm not pretending anything,' Emma persisted stubbornly, 'and for your information my presence here is none of your business. You're not my employer. Thank God.'

The car slowed down and pulled over to the side of the road.

'What do you think you're doing?' Emma's green eyes flashed angrily. 'Could you please get this car going?'

He turned to face her, and Emma edged away from him, feeling a ridiculous prickle of heat rush to her face. Under the thick black lashes, his bright blue eyes were staring intently at her, totally devoid of expression.

'Let's get a few things straight right now,' he ground out. 'First of all, what you're doing here is my business because I say it is. Secondly, I don't appreciate your tone of voice.'

'You don't appreciate my tone of voice!' She laughed incredulously, 'I don't appreciate yours much, either! So we're quits! And as for my presence here being your business—well, excuse me for seeming dense, but I can't see what it has to do with you at all! Or do you normally take such an interest in every employee that Alistair recruits?'

He leaned towards her, and she could feel the warmth of his breath on her face. There was something disturbingly sensual about him. It confused her, and Emma didn't like being confused.

She inched away sharply and his hand flicked out, catching her by the wrist. Emma twisted uselessly, finally giving up the fight.

'All right,' she said tightly, 'so you're stronger than me. But if you think that physical force is going to make me change my attitude towards you then you're wrong. You might be able to play the dictator with all those women who seem to have nothing better to do than flock around you, if the newspapers are anything to go by, but I'm not a member of your adoring flock, so I'll use any tone of voice I please with you. Now, if you'll kindly release me...'

He didn't release her, and Emma felt a swift stab of apprehension. Everything about Conrad DeVere was forbidding, from the taut, athletic grace of his body to the hard glint in his eyes. She wished that she hadn't argued with him. She should have just kept her big mouth shut and politely listened to whatever he had to say, and then just ignored him. It was what she would have done with any other man. She would have treated his words with contempt. But there was something about Conrad that sparked off all sorts of reactions in her.

'Are you going to listen to what I have to say, or do I have to resort to my own methods of persuasion?' His eyes roamed over her face and body, then back to her face.

Emma's eyes widened. She nodded. 'All right.' If he wanted to be a Nosy Parker, then who was she to argue? Nosy Parker, she thought, trying to derive some comfort from his diminished status. If only he were slightly less physically overpowering, she might just succeed in believing her description of him.

What, she wondered, did all those women see in him anyway? Personally, he was just the sort of man she loathed. She especially loathed the way that he was now examining her as though she were some distasteful species of insect under a microscope.

'I happen to be very fond of Alistair Jackson. He's been like a father to me for as long as I can remember, and I don't intend to see him fall prey to any potential gold-diggers.'

Emma's cheeks were burning. 'How dare you?'

'So, if that's what you have in mind, then you might just as well forget it, because you'll have me to contend with. He's already suffered at the hands of one woman after his bank balance; he doesn't need a repeat of the experience.'

His grip on her hand relaxed and Emma tugged it away, gently massaging the blood back into her veins.

So he thought she was a gold-digger! The idea would have been ludicrous if he weren't sitting there, inspecting her with menacing thoroughness.

'I don't know where you get your ideas from,' she said, controlling her temper with difficulty, 'but you're way off target. I heard of this job from a friend of a friend, and I applied. It's as simple as that. If you think I'm after Alistair Jackson's money, then you've got an overactive imagination.' She stopped to catch her breath, wishing she could sound more nonchalant and controlled.

'I help people write their biographies, Mr DeVere.' She uttered his name with exaggerated distaste and noticed with disappointment that he did not react. 'So I come into contact with the rich and famous quite a bit. I certainly wouldn't travel halfway across the globe to start my career as a gold-digger.' All right, so she didn't bump into the rich and famous on a daily basis, but the second half of her statement was the truth.

Conrad looked at her unhurriedly, his gaze starting from the top of her head and travelling slowly down her body. Then his eyes flicked back to hers.

'I made a point of doing a few checks on you when your application for this job was accepted,' he said smoothly. 'I found out some surprising facts.'

Emma's heart seemed to skip a beat. She licked her lips nervously, fighting to maintain some semblance of composure.

He couldn't have found out about her. Not that it wasn't possible, but it was unlikely. Not unless he knew what he was looking for. So, she thought, there was no reason to be worried. Nevertheless, under the folds of her skirt her fists unconsciously clenched and unclenched.

'Really?' She tried to sound only marginally interested. She couldn't afford to let a flicker of emotion cross her face. This man was no fool. If she wasn't careful he would be able to sense her anxiety at his words, and then where would she be? Apart from being clever—too clever—he struck her as the persistent type. He would dig and dig until all her carefully arranged plans were unearthed and scattered in ruins around her feet.

She threw him what she hoped was a careless, sunny smile, although her mouth ached with the effort of doing it. Why, she thought, couldn't he just vanish on the next flight out?

'Yes,' he said conversationally, restarting the engine and slowly pulling away from the grass verge. 'Would you like to hear what I found out?'

Emma looked at the dark, ruthless set of his features and shrugged. 'Would I be able to stop you?'

'You could always tell me that you're not interested. Wasn't that your stand a few minutes ago?'

He laughed softly when she didn't say anything, and her teeth clamped together in anger. He was playing a cat-and-mouse game with her, and enjoying it.

She added 'sadist' to her list of descriptions of him.

'I wish you'd get to the point,' she said.

'Well, the point is, Emma—do you mind if I call you Emma? The point is,' he carried on, without waiting for an answer from her, 'that I know quite a few people in your line of work, and my contacts have informed me that over the past eight months you passed up three offers of a job, all working with some very prominent people. I was told that you had something else in the pipeline. To be specific, this job. So what I want to know is, why? If you're as free of any underhand motives as you claim to be, why turn down Rome and Hong Kong in favour of an island?'

Emma relaxed. He hadn't found out about her. She was stupid to have panicked at all.

'There you go,' she crowed triumphantly. 'If I were a gold-digger, I would have snapped up one of those offers.'

'Except that Alistair is the oldest, and by far the wealthiest.'

His vivid blue eyes met hers, and she could almost feel him trying to unlock her mind and unravel her most personal secrets.

No wonder, she thought, he was such a big deal in business. Even knowing that she was safe, she still felt a stab of wariness.

'That never even occurred to me,' Emma replied truthfully. 'I can't imagine what types you mix with, but you have a very jaded idea of women if you think that we're all after as much as we can get.'

'Are you normally so lippy?'

Emma flushed, feeling unreasonably offended by what she saw as an implied criticism of her. True, she always made a point of standing up for herself, but she had never seen it as a flaw in her character. Conrad made it seem as though it was a trait that wasn't particularly desirable in a woman. Just as well, she thought, that she couldn't care less what he thought.

'Is the interrogation finished?' she asked coldly.

'Doesn't the isolation of this island bother you?' Conrad continued as though she had not spoken. 'Don't you think that you might miss the bright lights?'

'I don't need the night life, if that's what you mean.' Unlike you, she added silently to herself. If the gossip columns were anything to go by, Conrad DeVere never slept.

A little voice told her that gossip columns did not exactly adhere to the truth like glue to tissue paper, but she ignored it.

'Funny,' he mused with a sarcastic cut to his voice. 'You strike me as the sort of girl who would find the night life very exciting. After all, you're young, attractive...' He allowed the sentence to drift, the shrewd blue eyes glancing across at her.

Emma felt a twinge of alarm. She looked at him, suddenly oddly conscious of his masculinity. The heat, she thought, must be getting to her.

'And tired,' she finished hurriedly for him. 'How much longer before we get there?' He seemed to be driving abnormally slowly, although to be fair the roads were rough.

They had left the one and only stretch of highway behind, and were travelling across much smaller winding roads. On the one side, the dense mat of trees seemed intent on consuming the narrow strip of tarmac at the first opportunity; on the other the vista stretched across yet more thick forest until in the distance the water glimmered like sapphire.

'There's not much to do here,' Conrad persisted, treating her interruption with bland disregard. 'Won't you miss the theatres? And surely there's some young man waiting for you back in London?'

'That's none of your business.'

'As I told you, everything about you is my business.' His voice was soft and silky-smooth.

Emma didn't answer. She gazed through the window at the lush green panorama and wished that the man sitting beside her would simply evaporate in a puff of smoke.

While she had been arguing with Conrad she had had no time to feel apprehensive. Now that sick fluttering in her stomach was returning. They surely couldn't be very far away from Alistair Jackson's house now. Not that there was much evidence of civilisation around them.

Other cars were few and far between. There were no buildings or high-rise houses, only the occasional scattering of villages where groups of dark-skinned children played by the side of the twisting road, or else bathed under standpipes. They were obviously self-sufficient for food, because chickens clustered around the wooden huts, and glimpses of back yards showed that they cultivated all their own vegetables and fruit.

'We're nearly there.' Conrad's voice broke into her silent appreciation of the scenery, bouncing her back to the present.

'Good,' she lied. She wished now that she had never boarded that plane at Heathrow. What if she discovered that Alistair Jackson was a disagreeable, cantankerous old man? Wouldn't it have been better to have remained in England and continued to visualise him through conveniently distant rose-coloured spectacles? Reality was so often poles apart from what you thought it was going to be.

'What did you mean when you said that Alistair Jackson had been taken in by a woman who was after his money?'

Emma would have preferred not to talk to Conrad at all, but the only option open to her, of remaining silent, was too full of uncomfortable worries for her liking.

'Nervous?' he asked with an aggravating guess at the truth.

'No.' Emma glared at him. On top of everything else, the man was a mind-reader. 'I was simply trying to be polite. If it's too much for you, though...'

Conrad smiled, his first genuine smile of amusement, and she glimpsed that notorious charm which the newspapers were always going on about. A ridiculous warmth swept over her.

'Lisa St Clair. Ever heard of her?'

Emma shook her head.

'No. The newspapers never managed to get hold of the story. They would have had a field day if they had. Happened years ago. She came to Alistair highly recommended as a nurse, a very beautiful nurse, and with her mind on doing a bit more than mere nursing. I was only a teenager when it all happened, but my father told me that Alistair escaped by the skin of his teeth. Apparently this lady had an accomplice, a good-for-nothing wastrel whom she kept conveniently in the background. Someone saw them together in a hotel somewhere in Trinidad, and word somehow got back to Alistair. He wasn't pleased.'

'I can imagine. From the newspaper clippings I've read of him,' she mused aloud, 'I wouldn't have thought him the sort to fall for someone like that. I guess all hard-nosed tycoons must have their soft spots.'

'I guess we do.' Conrad looked at her with wry amusement and Emma blushed.

It must have been exhaustion after the hours spent on the plane and at the various airports, because her rigid self-control seemed all haywire. She was responding to things Conrad said in a way that was so out of character for her that Emma could only blame it on nerves and exhaustion.

'He'd been through a prolonged bad patch,' Conrad was saying. 'I was only a boy at the time, but apparently his daughter, his only daughter, left home against his wishes. Eloped with some fellow.'

Conrad was concentrating on the road. He didn't see Emma's face whiten.

'What do you know about it?' she asked casually, toying with the leather strap of her bag. 'I mean, it's useful finding out as much as I can about Alistair, and as from as many angles as possible, if my input is to be relevant.'

It sounded good. Believable. Emma wondered whether to enlarge on the reasons for wanting to know why Caroline Jackson had left home, and decided against it. There was no point in arousing Conrad's curiosity unnecessarily.

Conrad shrugged. 'Not much more to tell. She eloped and was never heard from again. Sank like the proverbial stone into a pond of water, and didn't leave a ripple behind her.'

Emma digested his summary of events in silence.

'Why didn't Alistair try to locate her?'

'How do you know that he didn't?' Conrad looked at her briefly through narrowed eyes.

'Just assumed,' Emma said hastily. 'I mean, if he had located her, they would be in contact now, wouldn't they?'

She made it sound like a statement of fact, rather than a question, and let the whole subject lapse into silence. Conrad was sharp enough to tune in to nuances of interest, and that was the last thing she needed.

The car was slowing down, turning away from the main road up an ever narrower side route, where the undergrowth, untamed and prolific on the main road, had here been trimmed back and given some semblance of order.

With a numb, prickly tension, Emma watched the large Jackson villa loom towards them.

It sat with majestic grandeur at the end of a long drive and an open courtyard, and in the middle of what Emma considered the finest gardens that she had ever seen.

The grass was trimmed to a crew-cut, and carefully landscaped with all manner of tropical foliage, from the bright colours of bougainvillaea to tall hibiscus bushes, sprouting red and yellow open-petalled flowers.

It was so much more breathtaking than she had expected, and the photographs which she had seen of it were spectacular enough.

So here I am at last, she thought wonderingly. The present meets the past.

Her hand trembled as she slid open the car door, to find Conrad looking at her curiously.

'He doesn't bite.'

'What?' Emma blinked at him.

'Alistair. He doesn't bite. Or do you normally get an attack of stage-fright every time you start a new assignment?'

'Yes,' Emma said, agreeing with whatever he had said. Her mouth had dried up and all she seemed able to manage were monosyllables.

Conrad was staring at her thoughtfully, but he didn't say anything.

He collected her suitcases and hold-alls, and walked to the front door, chatting amiably to the plump dark woman who opened it.

Emma followed and with every step she took her palms felt more clammy. She should never have come. She should never have come, because there were some things better left alone. She looked around at the Land Rover with a sense of yearning.

Around her, she heard the rich sing-song tones of the house help, Conrad's laconic drawl, the ticking of a grandfather clock.

It all washed over her. She started when Conrad asked her whether she wanted to see Alistair now or else later, after she had bathed.

'Now,' she managed to say. When he began walking beside her, she turned to him politely. 'You can just tell me where to go,' she said. 'I'm sure I'll be able to find my way.'

'I'm sure you would,' he replied blandly.

He continued walking with her, and Emma stopped in her tracks. 'Why are you coming with me?'

'Because,' Conrad drawled with infuriating shrewdness, 'I want to be there when you meet Alistair. You may have half convinced me that you're not a gold-digger, but you're still hiding something from me, and I'd like to find out what it is. I'm not used to people having secrets, not from me, at any rate.'

For a second Emma forgot her nervousness, and rounded furiously on Conrad.

'If I wanted a chaperon, I would have asked for one!' she snapped. 'Shouldn't you be heading back somewhere, anyway, now that you're through cross-examining me? Don't you have work to do? Companies to run?'

Conrad was clearly amused by her display of anger. He smiled, and Emma resisted the temptation to knock out his front teeth.

'I'm touched by your concern for the welfare of my companies in my absence, but I think they can do without me for a few days.'

'A few days?'

Emma stared at him in dismay. The man unsettled her. She was in a delicate enough situation as it was; the last thing she either wanted or needed was to have him hovering around, making her feel things that she was not used to feeling and didn't much like.

'The study's just here at the end of the corridor.' He walked off, and Emma hurried after him. Since she'd arrived, she seemed to have spent most of her time hurrying after the damned man. With her mouth drawn in a tight line, she waited while he knocked and then pushed the door open.

'Alistair,' he said, 'I have your writer, Emma Belle.'

Alistair Jackson sat in his wheelchair, surrounded by shelves of books. Emma followed Conrad into the large room, her eyes fixed on Alistair's face.

He looked older than she had expected, somehow more frail. Had he really once been so tall and proud? The hair, full and dark in the faded photograph which she had inspected so many times, had given way in old age to a high balding dome. Under thick brows the eyes were still young, however, and were scrutinising her intently.

She was aware of Conrad lounging by the window, but she could not prevent the curiosity from showing on her face.

Ever since her mother had told her about Alistair, when she had been very young, Emma had been curious about him, but it was only in the last few months, when the possibility of actually meeting him was on the horizon, that she had begun to build her careful, detailed picture of him.

She waited for him to speak, and when he did the depth of his voice surprised her. She listened to him as he shifted the conversation between Conrad and herself, chatting about generalities, and thought, He must have been quite something once. There was still an aura of command about him, even now.

Part of her responded to what he was now saying, asked the right questions, made all the right noises. The rest of her was slowly trying to reconcile him with the man whom her mother had feared and respected for so many years.

Slowly the tension began to ease out of her body. She could feel herself physically relax and begin to respond to his questions with less restraint.

When he asked her if the following morning would be too soon to start work, she responded enthusiastically, 'We could start this minute if you like!'

Alistair's firm mouth relaxed into a smile and he raised one restraining hand. 'I wouldn't hear of it. You've only just arrived. Spend the rest of the day unwinding. Believe me, you'll need some rest before we begin on my autobiography. The things I could tell you!'

His eyes clouded over and Emma remained silent. She wondered what was going through his mind. Was it her mother? The temptation to ask was almost irresistible, but she bit it back. Everything, she thought, would unfold in its own time and not a minute before.

'I'm sure,' Conrad drawled, 'that you're not the only one with stories to tell.' He looked at Emma with one raised eyebrow, and she scowled. She had almost managed to forget his presence.

'No,' she replied sweetly, 'I'm sure you have no end of stories that you could amuse us with.'

'Well, anyway——' Alistair looked at them narrowly, and then waved his hand '—no time for stories of any kind. An old man like me needs his beauty sleep.' He turned to Conrad with a grimace. 'You know how finicky that stupid doctor of mine is. He may even threaten to send that harridan of a nurse here again, and I don't think I could cope with the experience twice in a lifetime. It's bad enough that he sees fit to deprive me of my beloved whisky, and the occasional cigar, but——' and he turned to face Emma '—if you saw that battleaxe of a matron, then you'd really understand the meaning of suffering.'

He chuckled, but Emma suddenly noticed that he was looking tired. When he rang the bell for Esther to take him to his room, she stood up, realising with a start from a glance at her watch that they had been talking for far longer than she had thought.

'Conrad can show you around the house and grounds,' Alistair said from the door.

'I'd prefer to show myself around,' Emma began, but Alistair was already out of the room.

She turned to collect her handbag from where it was slung over the arm rest.

'No guided tour?' Conrad asked in a mocking voice.

'I'd rather go on a guided tour with a python.' To Emma's annoyance, he burst out laughing, and she reluctantly grinned. She looked at him and for a split second their eyes locked. Something in his expression made her turn away first, her heart pounding in her chest.

'I have unpacking to do anyway,' she said breathlessly, moving towards the door and keeping as much distance between them as she possibly could.

He moved towards her and Emma looked at him in dismay, her body responding with infuriating sensitivity to his nearness. She would have left the room, she had every intention of doing so, but her feet refused to obey the commands from her brain. They remained firmly planted on the ground until Conrad was so close to her that she could feel his warm breath on her face when he spoke.

'And I was hoping to find out what you're trying so desperately to hide.'

'Hide?' Emma laughed unconvincingly. 'I'm exhausted, that's all.'

'Well,' he said smoothly, 'I'm here for a couple of days more. Time enough for you to overcome your . . . exhaustion.'

This time Emma did flee, walking quickly towards the door and making sure that she shut it firmly behind her.

Esther showed her to her bedroom, but it was only when she was inside that she felt her body sag as all the nervousness and anxiety drained out of her.

Alistair, she thought, was at least not the cantankerous old man that she had dreaded. He was forceful but approachable, and with a biting but very witty sense of humour. In fact, Emma decided, he was endearing.

She sat on the bed, and pulled a sealed letter out of her bag, staring thoughtfully at the black, rounded writing on the front.

Eighteen months ago her mother had given her the letter, and told her to give it to Alistair, to hand-deliver it, to make peace for her as she couldn't do it herself.

Two days later she had died.

Emma carefully slotted the envelope underneath her make-up tray in the top drawer of the dressing table. She ran a bath, even though she knew that a shower would have been much quicker, and relaxed in the warm water for half an hour, turning over the events of the past few hours in her head.

Of course, Alistair was the only reason that she was here. Conrad had been right when he'd guessed that she did not need the job, but had taken it for a very specific reason.

With unwelcome obstinacy her mind threw into focus a graphic picture of him—raven-haired, arrogant, with the same caustic sense of humour as Alistair, except that there was an element of danger to him that was not there in the old man.

He was definitely a complication on the scene. Emma stood up and began rubbing herself vigorously with one of the towels.

She tried to squash all thoughts of Conrad DeVere, but they kept popping up with aggravating regularity.

In prospect, it had all been so straightforward. She would come to the island, with the very legitimate excuse of working for Alistair, and that way she would be able to find out all about him. It was what her mother had wanted.

Most importantly, she would be able to do it incognito.

She dressed slowly, her eyes wandering over the bedroom, appreciating the attention to detail of the décor, and the stunning view overlooking the gardens.

She reasoned that Conrad's appearance was nothing to worry about. He did not know who she was, and he was only going to be around for a couple of days at the most, anyway. She would simply avoid him, and concentrate all her energies on getting to know Alistair. That was why she had come in the first place, for heaven's sake.

She shuddered as she thought what Conrad would say if he found out her true identity. She had felt him trying to unravel her secret, using all his powers of hypnotic persuasiveness, but he had been way off target.

How could he possibly even begin to guess that Caroline Jackson, that shadowy figure who eloped with an undesirable man all those years ago—twenty-three to be exact—was her mother?

And what would he think if he found out? The worst. He was a formidable businessman. Hardly the sort who was overflowing with the milk of human kindness. She thought back to his attitude towards her and decided that he definitely was not the sort who was overflowing with the milk of human kindness. There was no question but that he would assume she had made this trip for her own ulterior motives. The man, she thought, was naturally suspicious and aggressive with it.

Emma lay on the bed and closed her eyes, the weariness of the last twenty-four hours catching up with her. She made a determined effort to shut Conrad DeVere out of her mind.

Alistair had at least been a pleasant surprise. Perhaps he had mellowed over the years. Her mother certainly had. Towards the end, she had spoken about her father with regret.

'It was all a mistake,' she had once told Emma. 'I ran away because I felt claustrophobic and I wanted adventure. Your father seemed to provide that adventure. He was everything Dad disliked. Wild, unstable, penniless. The worst part was that your grandfather was right. He was no good. He cleared off the minute I became pregnant with you.'

She had been too proud ever to return to the family home and admit that she had made a mistake. If she had, things might have been quite different.

If she had, Emma thought, I wouldn't be lying here trying to push unwelcome images of Conrad out of my mind.

She groaned in annoyance as her mind raced back to the unpleasant scene of him accusing her of being a gold-digger.

What on earth did all those women see in him, anyway? True, he had money and he was good-looking, but any fool could take one look at him and know that he was not the settling type.

So why did the mere thought of him make her feel hot and bothered? There were more important things at hand for her mind to become cluttered up with some man.

It was just a good thing that he wouldn't be around for much longer.

In the meantime, there was a lot for her to think about.

CHAPTER TWO

THE following two weeks were busy.

Because the days dawned earlier and brighter than in London, Emma found herself awakening before seven in the morning. Already at that hour the skies were blue and the sun was warming up in preparation for the intense heat which it would exude by midday.

She would normally have thought it a shame to waste the finest hours of the day cooped up in a study, but working with Alistair, apart from being of personal interest to her, was exciting as well. For an old man, Emma thought, with health problems, his dynamism was still formidable. He began the day at eight promptly and finished at one. Those five hours, Emma discovered, were utilised to the utmost.

'I'll be wizened and grey-haired at the end of this job,' she had laughingly told him on their second morning. 'I've met people a quarter of your age who haven't got your kind of stamina.'

Naturally the old man had been pleased and, to Emma's delight, tickled pink. Perhaps, she thought, her mother had found Alistair's energy and thirst for perfection simply too difficult to handle. As he described to her the dawnings of his rise from rags to riches, she glimpsed a man with a will of iron. There was little room in him for vulnerability, and maybe he saw the expression of love for his daughter as an area of weakness from which he shied instinctively.

All hypothesis. And anyway, Emma wondered, did it matter so much? She only knew that she was beginning to really like Alistair, to be fond of his ways and mannerisms.

He could be peculiarly thoughtful. It was a side to him which Emma found strangely touching. Coffee was always brought through to them at least once, accompanied by a plate of home-made cakes, which he insisted that she partake of.

'We can't have you wasting away, can we?' he joked. 'Besides, you're much too slim.'

'I don't think there's any danger of my wasting away,' Emma replied, casting her mind back to Esther's superb cooking. 'I haven't eaten so well in months.'

'No one to look after you, then?'

From anyone else the question would have been too intrusive for Emma's liking. From Alistair she took it as something of a compliment. From what she read between the lines, he did not extend his friendship lightly.

When she responded with a laugh that she was all alone in the world, his eyes lit up for a split second, but he did not pursue the topic.

'I hope you don't find my pace of work too demanding?' he asked, as he gathered up his notes at the end of the morning.

Emma looked up at him. 'Just the opposite,' she replied truthfully; 'it's invigorating. On my last assignment, my employer had an unnerving habit of drifting off into hours of digression, and at the end of the day we would have a page or two of worthwhile substance to show for hours of work. I like the way you can concentrate on the important issues.'

'Flatterer.' He looked at her craftily. 'I taught Conrad everything I know. He's very much like me in a lot of respects. Works hard, that young man.'

'Mmm,' Emma murmured non-committally. She had managed to put Conrad to the back of her mind over the past few days.

As far as she was concerned, it was the best place for him, and she was determined that he would stay right there, and not intrude on her thoughts as he had done when they had first met.

'I suppose you know that he's quite a bigwig in the business world,' Alistair pursued.

'Mmm.' Emma obligingly altered the tone of her murmur, but she refused to be drawn into a discussion on him.

'Some say that he's relentless.'

'Do they?' I can think of quite a few other words to describe him, she thought to herself grimly.

'What did you think of him?' Alistair shot her another crafty look which he attempted to camouflage under the guise of guilelessness.

'I don't know him.'

'You know what they say about first impressions.'

Emma shrugged and said airily, 'He seemed the relentless sort.' And that's putting it mildly, she added to herself.

'Well, you'll get to know him a bit better,' Alistair informed her. 'He may have mentioned to you that he's going to be staying here for a while?'

'Well, he did say something of the sort, but...' But she had seen nothing of him for the past few days, and she had assumed that any such idea had been aborted. She had *hoped* that any such idea had been aborted. At the mere thought of him, she could feel her pulses begin to race. Damn man!

'But?'

'Well, he hasn't been around, so I thought that he'd decided against it. I thought he'd decided that someone with an empire to run couldn't afford the time off.'

'Everyone needs a rest now and then.'

'Do they?' Emma couldn't resist a touch of sarcasm. 'He struck me as the sort who ran on overdrive one hundred per cent of the time.'

Alistair chuckled delightedly. 'A girl with spunk. I like that. That's what...' He halted in mid-sentence and looked away. 'Those women Conrad goes out with—bubbleheads, the lot of them. I've met more animated Barbie dolls in my time.'

'Perhaps that's why he goes out with them,' Emma said coolly. 'Maybe he thinks that any woman with half a brain cell would be unfair competition for him.'

She was alarmed at the sudden twist in the conversation, and even more alarmed that the mere thought of Conrad DeVere and his love life was enough to make her ruffled.

Alistair laughed out loud with glee. 'I hope you tell that to him at the first possible opportunity!' he said.

'There won't be a first possible opportunity,' Emma informed him. 'I see no reason why our paths should cross, except possibly at mealtimes.' And even then, she thought, lengthy discussions won't be on the agenda. I'd rather chat to a boa constrictor.

She had begun stacking her work into piles for typing after lunch when Alistair interrupted her.

'Leave it.' He gestured magnanimously. 'Tomorrow's Saturday. You can deal with all that typing some time over the weekend. Why don't you go to the beach this afternoon. Have you been there yet?'

'Not for a swim, no.' She had walked along it in the evenings, paddling in the water and thinking that heaven must surely be a slice of this island. At dusk, the little private cove was so quiet that she could hear herself think.

'Tut, tut, tut. You must think me a slave-driver. I insist you go to the beach as soon as lunch is out of the way. In fact, I could get Esther to bring something down for you. There are coconut trees that you could eat under.'

'No, really, it's...'

'Nonsense.' He waved aside her objections. 'I'd accompany you for a short while, but my health——'

'I know,' Emma chipped in with a laugh, 'your doctor, his instructions. When is Conrad due here, then?' she asked with as much nonchalance as she could muster, her hand on the doorknob.

Alistair mumbled under his breath, 'Oh, some time over the weekend, I should think. Tomorrow, probably.'

Better make the most of the rest of today, Emma thought to herself as she slipped into her bikini.

She had brought over a selection of swimwear and chose the style which she thought was least unflattering to her still pale complexion. The thought of a few hours on the beach, with nothing but a paperback for company, was delicious. What with one thing and another, she had not been on holiday for quite some time, and she had not been outside Europe for even longer.

Her mother had tried to encourage her to take a trip to Florida some years ago, but Emma had refused. It had seemed such a lot of money which could have been used on other, less self-indulgent things.

How her mother would have relished the thought of her now in Tobago.

In fact, Emma thought, as she skipped down the rocky incline to the cove, her mother would have been pleased at how naturally she got along with her grandfather. It might have compensated for her own stubborn pride and refusal to see him for all those years.

She laid the towel close to some coconut trees and abandoned herself to the sheer bliss of lying prone under the sun.

With the heat at its height, she could feel it pricking against her skin. She half opened her eyes and, glancing around the deserted beach, carefully undid her bikini-top, resting it conveniently within arm's reach, although there was practically no danger of anyone else coming on to the beach. The house and grounds, Alistair had told her on their very first day, was simply too remote to invite casual passers-by. The actual cove itself was even more secluded, set as it was down an incline and totally hidden from prying eyes.

Emma looked lazily out at the sea, turquoise and clear. The soft lapping of the ripples along the sand was soporific and soothing. It would be easy to fall asleep, she thought, and emerge three hours later looking like a lobster. It wouldn't be a pretty sight. She slapped on another layer of suntan oil and ran down to the water-line, treading cautiously at first, then, as her body adjusted to the temperature of the sea, splashing in, swimming languorously away from the beach.

No wonder people came to islands such as these and never left. The hubbub of London city life seemed more than thousands of miles away. It seemed like light years away.

Emma lay back, floating on the water, her eyes half shut. The gentle swelling of the water under her was the closest thing she could imagine to lying on a vast water-bed. She folded her arms behind her head, delighted to find that she did not immediately sink to the bottom as she had expected.

A wet slap on her stomach made her eyes shoot open.

When Conrad resurfaced a moment later there was the lazy glint of enjoyment in his eyes.

'What the hell are you doing here?' Emma yelled furiously. With desperate, splashing movements she tried to shield her bare breasts from him without drowning at the same time. 'How long have you been around? Don't you have anything better to do than to prowl around scaring people?'

She was puffing and panting and all too aware that her face was probably blotchy and red as well. He, on the other hand, was calmly treading water, an amused smile on his lips.

'Did I disturb you?'

Emma felt her body burn as he lazily inspected her frantic movements.

'No! Of course not!' she shouted, her green eyes flashing with anger, 'I always enjoy people sneaking up on me and frightening me to death!'

She began swimming purposefully back to shore, realising with dismay that Conrad was keeping up with her, his bare brown arms cutting swiftly through the water.

'Shall I turn my back like a true gentleman?' he asked as they approached the beach, his mouth curving in what looked suspiciously like a grin.

'I'd appreciate it!' Emma snapped back. 'And if you're any kind of gentleman you'll swim right back out to sea and continue swimming until you reach some other island! And if I see you struggling, don't count on me to send help!'

She could hear him laughing as she walked towards her bundle of clothes. Her hands were trembling with anger as she slipped on her bikini-top, only managing to snap together the fastening clasp with difficulty.

She sat stiffly on her towel, watching him as he stood on the water's edge and ran his fingers through his wet hair. Damned if he was going to drive her off the beach and back up to the house. She had been enjoying herself until he came along, and she had every intention of continuing to do so. She would simply ignore him. She lay on her back, annoyed with herself for continuing to watch him as he walked towards her.

He moved with a lithe and curiously pleasing grace. Even from a distance there was something dangerously attractive about him. Emma firmly shut her eyes, trying to stifle a prickle of awareness.

'Mind if I join you?' she heard him ask from somewhere over her.

'Yes.'

He ignored her and tossed his towel alongside hers, stretching down slowly on to it.

Emma glanced at him covertly out of the corner of her eyes. Tiny droplets of water remained on his bronzed body, trickled from his hair on to his forehead. With his eyes half closed, she noticed, his eyelashes were long and black but, against the angular planes of his face, not in the slightest feminine. If anything, they emphasised his disconcerting physical sensuousness.

'You seem to have made quite a hit with Alistair,' he drawled without looking at her.

'We're getting along well, if that's what you mean,' Emma replied coolly, refusing to be drawn into an argument with him.

'I left him singing your praises.'

'He appreciates efficiency and my typing speeds are well above average.'

She turned round to find Conrad's fierce blue eyes fixed on her. As her eyes rested briefly on his mouth, alarm bells began ringing in her head and she looked away.

She would be stupid if she did not find Conrad attractive. Everything about him was put together in a way that almost screamed sexuality. But there was no way that she would allow herself to be attracted to him.

'I was under the impression that you weren't due here until tomorrow,' she said tersely.

'Were you? I told Alistair that I would be down today. In fact, Esther's already prepared my room for me.'

Emma wondered whether Alistair had forgotten. It wasn't like him, but everyone was allowed their fair share of memory-lapses.

'Disappointed?' he asked.

With a swift movement, he sat up and regarded her with cool eyes. Emma glared at him. She had had an unexpected thought. Perhaps his sudden craving for rest and relaxation at Alistair's house had its origins in a desire to keep his eye on her, to make sure that she didn't throw off her well-schooled and aloof front the minute his back was turned, and revert to the gold-digging vamp which he had assumed she was.

The thought was not pleasing, and Emma immediately began to feel her hackles rise. Why else would his opening remark be an observation on how well she got along with Alistair?

'I'm merely surprised that you decided to take a holiday when the world of big business is out there, no doubt struggling without you at the helm.'

Emma saw his mouth tighten with anger and was inexplicably ashamed of her sarcasm.

'You obviously have over-inflated ideas about my influence.'

Emma was silent for a while. 'I just thought that you were joking when you said you would be coming to stay with Alistair,' she finally admitted.

'I rarely say something unless I mean it.' Conrad's voice was smooth and razor-sharp. 'The world is already too full of people shooting their mouths off for no reason other than that they like the sound of their own voices. Alistair at least avoids that particular vice. When he speaks, he has something to say, something worth listening to.'

'Definitely,' Emma agreed.

She hoped that he would go away. Lying prone, she felt too conscious of his eyes on her and couldn't relax.

'Island life agrees with you,' Conrad said lazily. She felt his finger brush against her thigh and pulled away sharply.

'What are you doing?'

'There was a sandfly on your leg,' he said, with an expression of mock innocence. 'Do you normally jump a mile high when someone touches you?'

Emma glared at him. The spot where his finger had rested still burned as though he had ignited a tiny flame underneath her skin. She looked at his fingers with disdain.

'Do you normally inflict your company on other people, when they clearly would rather be alone?' she asked coldly, ignoring his question.

'Most people don't view my company as a burden,' he said in a matter-of-fact voice, fixing his azure eyes on hers until Emma felt as though she was being mesmerised by a snake charmer.

Her heart was thumping in her chest and her mouth felt dry. What on earth is the matter with me? she thought. Could it be the heat? She didn't think she had been sitting in the sun for that long.

'Especially those of the opposite sex,' he continued, with a hint of lazy amusement in his voice.

'Well, there's no accounting for taste,' Emma bit out. His words had evoked an erotic picture of Conrad's lean, bronzed body and she tried to sweep it out of her mind like so much unwelcome dust under a carpet. Were there no limits to this man's ego? She was tempted to tell him that power and good looks had clearly gone to his head, but she resisted.

Instead she threw him a look of scorn, noticing that it did not diminish the half-languid smile playing on his lips.

'How about you?' he asked, lying on his side to face her, so closely that she was embarrassingly aware of his warm breath on her face.

'How about me?'

'You've told me that you're not interested in the bright lights. Is there some quiet, retiring young man patiently waiting back in England for you?'

'You already asked me that.'

'I know. You never answered.'

'Yes, I did. I told you that my private life is none of your business!' Emma faced him. Up close, she saw that the blue of his eyes was speckled with very dark grey. She felt unsteady for the briefest of moments, and looked away.

'I suppose that means that there is some forlorn fool awaiting your return. If I were your boyfriend, I'd make sure that you didn't stray too far. With a tongue like yours, you could land yourself in all sorts of trouble.'

'Well, you're not, and for your information there's no forlorn fool waiting for me either in England, or anywhere. Now could you find another spot on the beach to sit on?'

Conrad looked at her curiously, as though she were some new and different species of life which he had not run into before.

'How do you occupy your time when you're not working with Alistair?' he asked, changing the conversation, much to Emma's relief.

'I type,' she said abruptly. 'Alistair persuaded me to forget about work this afternoon and come down here instead.'

'Did he, now?' Conrad said thoughtfully. He stretched back on his towel, his hands clasped behind his head, and contemplated the sky. 'Alistair's always been fond of his games,' he muttered.

'I beg your pardon?'

'Nothing. Absolutely nothing.' He stood up, flexing his legs. 'I think I'll go up to the house now. Coming?'

'No. I'll stay down here for a while longer.' She looked at him pointedly. 'I might be able to enjoy the peace and quiet.'

'Suit yourself.' He looked down at her, his eyes casually running the length of her body. 'Be careful of the sun, though. Too much and you'll end up looking like something that's crawled out from the bottom of the sea.'

Emma sat up angrily as he turned and began walking off towards the rocky path that led back up to the gardens.

Dammit! Didn't that man have anything pleasant to say? True, he had only said what she herself had thought only a short while before, but nevertheless she resented his tone of voice. It was far too smug for her liking.

She hoped that he would trip over some of the rocks and come crashing back down to the beach. Nothing serious, just enough to wipe that clever, arrogant smile from his lips.

She followed his figure and saw him clamber lithely over the rocks and vanish towards the house.

Her serene enjoyment of the beach had evaporated. She lay on her towel for another fifteen minutes, her mind treacherously playing back images of Conrad and her own defensive, irrational response to him.

She fervently hoped that his little holiday on the island would be limited to a few days. She might be able to keep her temper in check for a few days, but, if he stayed much longer, then she would be bound to give way sooner or later. Something about him rubbed her up the wrong way, and, she acknowledged frankly, it had nothing to do with the fact that he probably still suspected her motives for being here in the first place.

No. It was something more fundamental than that. Everything about him nettled her.

Still, she thought with a twist of amusement, it must be quite a shock to his system to find that not every available female with twenty-twenty vision swooned at his feet.

She gathered up her belongings and headed for the house. Neither Alistair nor Conrad were to be seen. Alistair might possibly still be resting, but Conrad? Probably lurking around somewhere. He didn't seem the sort to be happy sitting still for too long.

Rather than take her usual shower, Emma ran a bath, copiously squirting bubble bath into the tub, and sank into the water with a sigh of bliss.

She was not looking forward to dinner in the evening. Normally she dined simply with Alistair, and they spent an hour or so afterwards conversing about ground that they had covered during the day, or whatever else came into their heads.

So far no mention had been made of her mother, and Emma was content to let the subject ride until the appropriate opportunity arose.

With Conrad now on the scene, she seriously doubted that such an opportunity was likely to arise, and that irritated her yet further.

She took her time dressing, slipping into an apricot sleeveless dress and her flat leather sandals. She had acquired the first golden shimmer of a tan and, against her pale gold colour and the apricot dress, her hair seemed startlingly blonde.

If blondes, she thought, staring at her reflection in the mirror, were supposed to be vivacious and giggly, then she certainly disproved the theory. Inside, she felt, was a brunette struggling to get out.

Her mother had been dark, her hair tinged with red, the colour of chestnut, and she had jokingly banned her daughter from ever taking a bottle of dye to her hair. A natural blonde, she had told Emma, was a rare species, and she should be thankful.

Emma wondered whether Conrad would have been so accusatory towards her if she had had dark hair. Maybe not. He might just have taken her more seriously from the start, or never even suspected her of anything in the first place.

She forced her thoughts away from him, and made her way slowly towards the living-room area, where a glass of sherry would be awaiting her. It had become a routine which she enjoyed.

Alistair was sitting in his usual position by the french doors which opened out on to the huge expanse of the garden.

Conrad, with his back to her, looked around as she walked in, meeting her stony glance with an ironic smile.

He was dressed in a pair of beige trousers and a short-sleeved grey-blue shirt which did very little to hide the broad width of his shoulders and his long, muscular legs.

'I see you took my advice about overstaying your welcome in the sun,' he remarked casually, inspecting her with the sort of slow thoroughness which had made Emma bristle on the very first day they had met.

'Actually, I had arrived at the same conclusion myself,' Emma said politely. 'It doesn't take a genius to work out that too much sun isn't a good idea.'

'Slowly but surely does it,' Alistair chipped in, his shrewd eyes glancing between them. 'You've acquired just the right shade of pale brown. You look quite fabulous. Doesn't she look fabulous, Conrad?' He looked ingenuously at Conrad, who seemed about to say something, only to have second thoughts.

'Fabulous,' he repeated drily, then switched his attention to Alistair, resuming the conversation which Emma supposed they had been having before she walked in.

Oh, charming, she thought, wondering why on earth she was disappointed to be excluded when to be excluded was better than to be subjected to a barrage of barely veiled criticisms.

She picked up her glass of sherry and sat on the sofa next to Alistair, listening to them and gradually becoming enthralled at their discussions.

When Conrad spoke, it was with a vigour and a command of knowledge which somehow came as no surprise. He discussed worldwide market trends, and their effect on Alistair's holdings, with a perception and shrewdness which she assumed had made him such a force in business.

Over the meal, a West Indian speciality of cooking bananas, Creole rice and fish stewed in coconut, the conversation switched to more general topics, and Emma found herself joining in.

Neither Conrad nor Alistair had been to London for several months, and they quizzed her about the theatres and the operas. Emma animatedly described as much as she could, from, she admitted, reviews and information gleaned from the newspapers rather than first-hand experience.

'The theatre I go to as often as I can,' she confessed, 'but the opera—well, that's quite a different matter. The prices tend to be way out of my league. I was invited a couple of times and I thoroughly enjoyed myself, but I have yet to make it on my own.'

'Who did you go with?' Conrad asked casually. 'An opera buff?'

'Oh, a friend,' Emma replied smoothly, steering the conversation away from herself and into less personal waters. Two glasses of sherry and a glass of port might have relaxed her a little, but certainly not enough to let slip anything revealing about herself.

She had always been careful about sharing confidences, preferring to keep her life to herself. Now it had become almost second nature, a habit to which she adhered almost without thinking.

Perhaps it was a character trait which she had somehow gleaned from her mother. When her mother had settled first in Coventry, then in London, she had always managed to keep her private life to herself, confessing to none of her friends anything about her background.

'They can take me as they find me,' she had once told Emma. 'My privacy is the one thing I cherish above all else.' She had laughed. 'Apart from you, my darling.'

Perhaps her obsession with privacy had stemmed first from her desire to conceal her whereabouts from her father.

There was no doubt that, as far as Alistair went, she had sunk without a trace.

Emma wondered whether he had ever tried to find her mother and thought not. Anger would have stopped him to start with, and then after that pride would have stepped in. Although, she thought honestly, her mother's pride, from what she had gleaned from Alistair's occasional throwaway remarks, had been far fiercer and deeper than his had ever been.

She had lived with the scars of her own mistakes, and had found it as impossible to forgive her father as she had to forgive herself. She would have erected enough barriers around her to have repelled the most insistent searcher.

Or maybe, she thought with a flash of intuition, Alistair *had* searched, and *had* found her, but had chosen not to intrude. In which case, he would have known about the existence of a granddaughter.

Did he? No, she convinced herself, although... although he treated her with the warmth of someone who delighted in her company far more than if she were merely his assistant. He could easily have checked her identity if he knew what he was looking for...

But no, she was just being over-imaginative. She frowned at him and brushed aside the thought, flicking it to the back of her mind like an irritating intrusion.

When she dragged herself back to the present, it was to find Alistair looking at her.

'Penny for your thoughts, my dear. We seemed to lose you there for a moment.'

Emma looked at him seriously. 'They're not worth a penny,' she said.

'What about a pound?' Conrad was staring at her, and Emma could almost see his brain clicking, trying to work out her secrets, trying to out-think her.

'Not much use on an island where dollars are the currency, is there?' She laughed awkwardly, suddenly feeling as though she were treading on quicksand.

The uncomfortable moment passed and Alistair was ringing his bell for Esther to take him to his bedroom.

'I'll leave you two to carry on,' he said, moving towards the door. 'Esther, bring through some more coffee for Emma and Conrad after you've taken me up.' He could already see Emma beginning to protest and waved aside her objections. 'You two have much more in common than you think,' he observed with a gesture. 'You should get to know each other better.'

'Alistair...' Conrad said in a warning voice, 'You're getting too old to play games.'

'Games? Son, I don't know what you're talking about. I merely feel obliged, as your host, to see that you get along and are enjoying yourselves.'

As he left the room, Emma heard him call over his shoulder, 'Besides, Conrad, I'm sure you'll want to tell Emma all about your fiancée. After all, they'll be thrown together soon enough, won't they?'

CHAPTER THREE

'YOUR fiancée?' Emma repeated incredulously. Why, she thought, was she so surprised, for heaven's sake? Wouldn't it be much more unusual if he *didn't* have a fiancée? She had read often enough about all those women who swarmed around him. A fiancée was the logical conclusion. In fact, it was surprising he wasn't married off by now.

Still, she felt a stab of pain and immediately composed her features into polite interest. She didn't like the man, wasn't interested in him at all apart from as a potential threat; she surely couldn't really give a damn if he was engaged, married, or widowed with ten children?

He was looking at her closely, his lips tightened into a grim line.

'Alistair has a knack of being indiscreet when he chooses.'

'Indiscreet? Why? Surely it's no big secret? I mean, isn't an engagement a cause for celebration?' She stared through the window behind him, not allowing a ripple of emotion to cross her face.

'For the moment, it's very much something of a secret. The newspapers would love to get their grubby little hands on a story like this, and that's the last thing I want.'

He ran his fingers distractedly through his hair, then sat heavily on the sofa, stretching his long legs out in front of him.

Emma tried not to look at him at all. She still had that funny feeling in the pit of her stomach, as though she had suddenly dropped one thousand feet in mid air, only to find herself safely on terra firma after all.

She wondered what his fiancée looked like, and the rush of jealousy that struck her almost left her gaping in surprise.

Of course, a shocked inner voice told her, it's not jealousy, simply the suddenness of the revelation.

'Alistair doesn't like her,' Conrad was saying. 'He thinks she's shallow and he thinks that I'm planning to marry her for totally the wrong reason.'

'And are you?' Emma felt compelled to ask, heartily wishing she could simply drop the subject rather than pursuing it with such tenacious interest.

'Well, I'm marrying her because it suits me to do so. It's more of a business arrangement. It's a matter of opinion as to whether or not that constitutes the wrong reason.'

He did not elaborate on what kind of business arrangement, and Emma allowed the words to sink in.

Fascinated, she watched as he clasped his hands behind his head, wondering how it would feel to have them caress her. She shook her head to get rid of the thought. What was happening to her? She had always been so level-headed.

'A business arrangement? You make it sound like some sort of company merger. And how does your fiancée feel about this?'

'Believe me, it's mutual. She thinks that marriage would enhance her career, and that I would provide the passport to all the right places. Which, of course, I would.'

'Of course,' Emma agreed cynically. 'A match made in heaven. You provide the passport and she provides the businesses. I'm surprised everyone doesn't jump on the bandwagon and start getting married for all those practical reasons. It would certainly do away with the candlelit dinners and courtship.'

Conrad was looking at her intently. 'I wouldn't have thought you were a firm believer in love at first sight and thunderbolts from the skies with violin music in the background.' His lips twisted cynically. 'Isn't that only the stuff of movies?'

'I wouldn't know,' Emma replied coolly.

'Meaning that you haven't been swept off your feet as yet?'

'Meaning nothing.' She felt a slow flush creep over her. It was beyond her why she was arguing the point with him. She had always thought that marriage could quite happily exist as a business arrangement. 'I simply think that you can't treat something as emotional as love and marriage with such detachment. As though you're going out to buy a car.'

'Love? Who ever mentioned love? Though she *is* very beautiful.'

Emma didn't answer.

'I wish I could see what went on behind that cool exterior of yours,' Conrad murmured, his eyes running over her body and finally resting on her face. 'You were vibrant enough at the dinner table, when you were discussing politics, but the minute the topic becomes too personal you close up like a clam.'

'Really?' Emma feigned indifference, but she could feel her heart pounding.

'Yes, really. Why are you so secretive? You've got some ulterior motive for being here. Why don't you just come out with it and tell me what it is? I'll find out sooner or later, you know.'

'Why do you keep trying to pry into what's no concern of yours?'

'If only it were that easy.' His words were spoken so softly that Emma barely caught them. There was a brief, electric silence broken only by the sounds outside of crickets and frogs.

'I'm surprised Alistair objects to the...to your arrangement,' she said hurriedly, 'when...'

'When what?'

Emma stared at him, realising that she had dug a hole for herself.

'When he opposed his own daughter's marriage for just the opposite reason, namely that it had not been thought out thoroughly, that it was solely an affair of the heart.'

'Did he say that?'

'Yes.' It was too late now for her to try and remember whether he had told her that or not. That watchful curiosity was back on Conrad's face and she turned away, not wanting to meet the questions in his sharp blue eyes.

'He's changed. Maybe that's the very reason he's against my engagement. Anyway, he's right about one thing. You'll be meeting Sophia soon enough. Her parents own a house on the golf course near here. She's coming to stay for three weeks.'

'How nice.'

Sophia, she thought. What a name. Hardly conjures up the picture of an ambitious career woman.

'Is she a model?'

Conrad looked at her in surprise. 'As a matter of fact, she is. She does a bit of acting as well, but from what I've seen she's hopeless.'

'That's charitable of you.'

Conrad's sensuous mouth curved into a smile and he raised one mocking eyebrow. 'I'll say this for you: you do have a certain dry wit that I haven't found in too many members of the opposite sex.'

'Maybe you've been hanging around with the wrong members of the opposite sex,' Emma said, trying to stifle the spurt of pleasure his compliment had given her.

'Maybe I have. Would you say it's too late to remedy that?' His voice was low and warm. Suddenly the room felt hot, too hot for comfort, and tiny needles were pricking under her skin.

'Far too late,' she replied crisply. Perhaps she was imagining the speculative intimacy behind his words, or maybe he was playing some kind of game. Whatever, she would do well to remember that she could not afford to let her guard drop. Not for an instant.

Anyway, she had no intention of being his victim. She rose abruptly, tossing her hair behind her shoulders.

'Well, I think I'll hit the sack.' She yawned and threw him a courteous, slightly dismissive look. 'I want to be up early to finish some work.'

'On a Saturday? No beach?' he asked with an air of feigned innocence.

The implication behind his words was blatant enough, and Emma replied more hotly than she intended, 'No, no beach! So you can find someone else to do your sneaking up behind!'

She slammed the door on his low chuckle.

Their conversation was still jarring on her nerves the following morning, and she made a deliberate point of avoiding him. There seemed little use in courting another battle of words, with her, she admitted, coming out the loser; and, besides, there was the typing to do.

As she settled in front of the word processor in Alistair's office she eyed the pile of notes, some scribbled, some astonishingly coherent, with an expression of reluctance.

Alistair had retired with his book to the pool at the back of the house. He had invited her to sit with him, but she had refused. She was not in the mood for lazing in the sunshine, even though the prospect of three hours' worth of typing did not do a great deal for her either.

She flicked through the sheets of paper, but her thoughts kept returning to Conrad.

She felt that she had guessed accurately enough at his character when she had first met him. A powerful man, aware of his own sexual attraction to women, and not against using it when it suited his purposes. The fact that he was almost frighteningly clever as well made his charm all the more lethal when he decided to use it.

She should have been prepared to meet him with the stony indifference which would have protected her against all his barbs, especially as he had had no qualms about telling her precisely what he thought of her when they first met.

It annoyed her that, after all that, he had still managed to get under her skin, like some wretched virus she couldn't quite manage to shake off.

A couple of throwaway compliments from him, a few ambiguous remarks which she had most probably imagined, and she had been squirming like a gawky teenager on her first date. Good grief! He probably acted precisely the same when he was talking to his sixty-year-old female employees. She frowned in self-disgust.

Shouldn't the fact that he was engaged have made him more reserved? she wanted to know.

He had disappeared to meet Sophia from the airport. When she saw them together, she would probably be able to put it all into perspective. They would be holding hands and whispering sweet nothings into each other's ears, even if he did profess to be cynical about love, and she would be able to relax and treat him as an almost married man. Easy. She would be able to harness her emotions and get her mind under control as it always had been.

She slipped the disk into the word processor and began clattering on the keyboard, sifting through the disorder until what appeared on the screen before her made sense.

The tiny dark grey print on the paler grey screen was soothing. After a while, Emma could feel the tension begin to ease out of her and her concentration take over.

Reading over what she had done, she saw Alistair in a more detached manner, the young Alistair at any rate, the boy still struggling to become a man and make his fortune in the world.

As yet, they had only covered his very early years, before he met her grandmother, and long before they'd had her mother and his story began to weave into hers.

He had been single-minded even as a young man, with the sort of blinkered drive that ground obstacles into dust. Emma could see how his ambition could have blighted any relationship he might have had with her mother. Her mother had been a sensitive woman. Incomprehensible to someone like the young Alistair, whose thirst for success had no time for the fine, subtle swings of emotion.

How he had changed, Emma thought. The old man with whom she now worked bore only a shadowy resemblance to the hard young boy about whom she was writing.

She become so absorbed in her work that it was nearly midday the next time she glanced at her watch.

She looked through the window at a perfectly clear blue sky. Even though the office was air-conditioned, she could almost feel the sun beating down outside. In weather like this it was no wonder everyone moved in slow motion. She did now, as well.

She stretched with a lazy, cat-like movement. The thought of lounging around the pool was beginning to look distinctly tempting, and she packed away her files quickly, flicking them into order as she did so.

Alistair was still by the pool when she emerged half an hour later, wearing a modest flowered one-piece and a pale blue beach coat. He was sitting in the shade, fully dressed in a shirt and cotton trousers and wearing a hat.

'Doctor's advice,' he said, pointing to the hat. 'He's managed to get me off the drink and the cigarettes, and now he even dictates my wardrobe. Pretty soon he'll be telling me what television programmes I can and can't watch.'

Emma laughed, her green eyes crinkling. Esther had prepared snacks for lunch, and Emma bit into one of the pasties, catching the crumbs with one hand.

In between mouthfuls of food, she chatted to Alistair about work. All the time she found herself watching for Conrad, almost disappointed when there was no sign of him.

Probably locked up in a bedroom somewhere, she thought, making up for lost time with Sophia.

The thought was so distasteful that Emma pushed it aside and concentrated on the surroundings, half listening to what Alistair was saying, half drowsing in the heat.

'Lying there, for a moment, my dear, you reminded me of someone, but I can't for the life of me think who. In fact, over the past few days, something about you...your mannerisms... It'll come to me in time, I expect. Old age. Dulls the memory, you know.'

Alistair's words cut through the haze of her drowsiness, and Emma sat up, trying not to let any surprise flicker across her face.

For the past few weeks she had been lulled into a sense of security, appreciating Alistair's company, almost forgetting the blood tie between them. Almost forgetting the letter lying in the drawer upstairs.

'I can't think why I should remind you of anyone,' she said warily, propping herself up on one elbow, and avoiding his speculative gaze. The niggling suspicions rose their heads, and she stamped them down resolutely. 'My goodness, you very nearly woke me up. I was beginning to fall asleep here. It's so peaceful and quiet. When will Conrad be making a reappearance?'

It was a line of conversation which she did not want to explore, but from experience Emma knew that Alistair could be distracted easily by the mention of Conrad's name. He seemed as proud of him as if he were his own son. If the alternative was a trip down memory lane, with Alistair trying to plumb his memory for a recollection of her, then far safer to stick to discussing Conrad DeVere, however unappealing the subject was.

'Some time this afternoon. He's gone to meet that wretched woman at the airport. He'll probably bring her back here with him, though thankfully she's not actually staying here. She'll be at her parents' house.'

'Yes, Conrad told me.'

'He's been discussing her with you?' Alistair's bright eyes looked at her slyly. 'I didn't realise you two were on such confidential terms already. Not that I mind in the least. On the contrary.'

'We're not on confidential terms,' Emma corrected him firmly. 'In fact, we're not on any kind of terms at all, confidential or otherwise. In fact, he didn't tell me a thing about his fiancée apart from her name and where she was staying.'

'Weren't you curious about her?' Alistair probed.

'No,' Emma lied.

Alistair shot her a disappointed look. 'Well, she's no competition for you at all, my dear.'

'Competition? I'm not in competition with anyone for that man's attention!' Emma responded hotly. She scowled at Alistair and he chuckled.

Alistair was needling her and clearly enjoying her discomfort. Emma resisted the urge to stick her tongue out at him. Instead, she turned over on to her stomach and let her arms fall on either side of the red and white sun lounger. Out of the corner of her eye, she looked at Alistair, who still wore the remnants of a grin on his face.

'Don't think much of Sophia. Nice enough, but I don't think they're suited. Don't approve of this engagement one jot. Never have.'

'So Conrad said.'

'Ah!' He sounded like the cat that had just discovered the pot of cream. 'So you *were* chatting about her! I thought you said that you hadn't been?'

'You're incorrigible!'

They both laughed. Emma stood up, bending her head forward and scooping up her hair, quickly braiding it and securing it with a coloured elastic.

'I,' she said, making a face at him, 'am going for a swim!'

'Not to get away from me, I hope?'

'You flatter yourself!'

With a lithe movement she stood poised on the edge of the pool for a few seconds, then dived cleanly into the water, gasping as she felt its coldness on her body.

She was a good swimmer and she enjoyed it. It was the closest thing to total freedom of movement that she could imagine. In England she had shied away from the public swimming baths, finding them overcrowded in the summer and too unappealing in the winter.

Here, she was making up for lost time. She held her breath and swam, using deep strokes to cover the length of the pool. When she re-emerged into the air, she threw her head back, her eyes shut, her face lifted towards the sun with an expression of hedonistic enjoyment.

Yes, swimming pools in England, she thought, had a long way to go.

She opened her eyes and turned towards Alistair, her mouth open to shout out her pleasure to him.

With a sensation of stunned surprise, she turned instead to face Conrad and Sophia, both staring at her, while in the background Alistair waved, gesticulating at Sophia's back and raising his eyes to heaven.

Emma reluctantly swam to the side of the pool and pulled herself out.

'Typing all done?' Conrad asked in a faintly mocking tone of voice. 'Not that I wouldn't have come to rescue you from the word processor if you had still been there.'

'How gallant.' Emma looked at his lean, muscular body with a shiver of unwelcome awareness, then she turned her attention to Sophia who had reached out and was holding Conrad at the elbow.

From behind them Alistair did the introductions. Emma barely heard him. She was looking at Sophia, thinking that, if her name did not conjure up the picture of a career woman, then her face and body certainly didn't.

She was tall and seemed to be tanned all over. Even her hair, cut fashionably short, was bronzed and so were her eyes, a peculiar shade of brown-gold. She was wearing five or six bangles on her wrist and every time she moved her hand they jangled like tiny bells.

Emma decided that she found the noise irritating. She herself possessed almost no jewellery at all and could never understand other people's fascination with it.

'You were working?' Sophia addressed her, raising her eyebrows in surprise. 'In weather like this?' She turned to Conrad. 'Darling, do you hate me too much because I wouldn't dream of being quite so industrious?'

Good grief! Emma thought, reaching for her towel and trying to ignore the indulgent smile on Conrad's face. She dried herself vigorously and then wrapped the towel around her, sarong-style. She stretched out on the sun lounger alongside Alistair. Through semi-closed eyes, she watched Sophia discard her silk wrap and twirl seductively in front of Conrad, showing him every possible angle of her body, scantily wrapped in what Emma estimated couldn't have been more than a few inches of white Lycra.

'Delightful,' Conrad commented, standing back to appreciate her. His eyes flicked across to Emma and she yawned widely. Pure coincidence, but, seeing him frown, she grinned back and stretched out for her book.

'Well, I'll see you lot later,' Alistair said, allowing Conrad to help him into his wheelchair. 'Sophia, dear,

I can't imagine why you bother with a swimsuit. There's so little of it that you might just as well have spared yourself the expense and gone for the all-nude look instead. A lot cheaper.'

Sophia's teeth clamped together angrily and Emma stifled a laugh.

'Silly old man,' she muttered to Emma, sitting on the edge of her sun lounger.

'Anything but,' Emma disagreed coldly. 'He happens to be extremely clever.'

'Oh, I know,' Sophia agreed quickly, 'Still, brains aren't everything.' She threw Emma a knowing look which said it all.

They may not be all, Emma thought, but they help. Then she looked at Sophia and wondered whether they did after all.

Face it, she admitted to herself, the woman probably earns a thousand times more than you do, and she's certainly no Einstein.

'Conrad tells me that you're a model. I would have guessed,' Emma confessed honestly, 'if he hadn't said.'

Sophia looked pleased.

'You may have recognised me? I was on the cover of *Vogue* a couple of months ago.' She raised her chin slightly, her eyes narrowing against the sun, her movements poised and slightly artificial.

'I don't get much time for reading magazines,' Emma said, wondering what greater accolade there could be for a model than to appear on the front cover of such a reputable magazine. She thought with amusement that the only place her picture was ever likely to appear would be in a photo album.

'And what exactly do you do?' Sophia slipped a pair of large sunglasses over her eyes and directed her gaze to the flat surface of the pool.

'I type,' Emma replied succinctly, deciding that an elaborate job description would be guaranteed to bore someone like Sophia to tears.

'I once went to a secretarial college,' Sophia said off-handedly, 'I only lasted about a month and a half. The typing was all right, but the shorthand was too difficult. All those silly little symbols. I couldn't really get the hang of it at all. And I hated being surrounded by women! Anyway, I never could concentrate on anything for too long. Besides, modelling pays much more. Not that I need the money. I could quite adequately have kept going on my trust fund, and now that I'm about to marry Conrad, well...' She allowed the sentence to drift to a meaningful pause.

Emma wondered where the husband-to-be was. He seemed to have taken an inordinately long time dropping Alistair back to his room.

'You must be very excited about the wedding,' Emma volunteered, a little ashamed at the triteness of the remark. She was finding the conversation heavy going. For the first time, she wished desperately that Conrad would reappear.

'No, not really. I would quite happily have lived with Conrad, but he insisted on marriage. I think he's afraid that someone else might snap me up if we're not legally hitched.' She laughed, a deep, throaty laugh, and Emma thought sourly that even that sounded sexy. She could not have been a day over twenty, if that, but already with the self-confidence of someone quite accustomed to being the centre of attention. Every gesture she made proclaimed it.

She watched as Sophia delicately tested the water with one toe, then gradually eased herself into the pool. Why, she thought, did Alistair disapprove of the match? She, acidly, considered Conrad and Sophia to be perfectly suited.

'Well, what do you think?'

Conrad's deep voice behind her made her jump. He squatted down until his face was close to hers. Emma edged away and his blue eyes flickered with amusement.

'Think about what?' she countered icily, annoyed with him for the effect that he had on her. 'The weather? World politics? Religion?'

'Sophia.'

'Ah. As a matter of fact, she's not what I expected.'

'What did you expect? A gold-digger?'

'Like me?' Emma mocked.

'I never said that.'

'But you implied it.' For some reason she wanted an argument. She knew that she was being childishly aggravating, but something in her persisted.

'Let's get one thing straight, lady,' Conrad said grimly, 'OK, I admit I quizzed you when you first arrived, but you told me that you weren't after Alistair's money, and I believed you, if only in the absence of any evidence. It's obvious that you can't accept that.'

Emma looked at him dumbly. 'Sorry,' she muttered.

The sharp blue eyes raked over her face.

'I think you're being very unfair on Sophia. Are you sure that she knows that your idea of marriage to her is a business arrangement? A company merger?'

'Of course,' Conrad replied smoothly. 'As I said, it suits her as much as it suits me. Not that having her around wouldn't be a pleasure.' He shot Emma a quick, sideways glance. 'Isn't she most men's idea of physical perfection?'

'I wouldn't know!' Emma snapped, immediately regretting her burst of emotion, which she proceeded to cover under a veneer of indifference. 'But I'll take your word for it. You clearly have enough experience in that direction.'

Her fists clenched hard on the arms of the lounger. God, she thought, why on earth do I let this man bother me? She discarded the train of thought, because to pursue it might throw up a few questions to which she could not provide the answers.

She heard Sophia's lilting voice calling from the pool, and they both looked in her direction.

'I think you're being summoned,' Emma said sweetly.

'When it's by a beautiful creature like Sophia, I don't object,' Conrad replied with equal silkiness.

He moved with an almost mesmerising grace to the side of the pool, and then dived in. Emma watched his tanned body slice through the water and emerge alongside Sophia.

He said something to her, and she laughed, throwing back her head and exposing the slim column of her neck. Conrad's lips trailed across the fine skin and Emma looked away.

It doesn't take a thousand guesses to hit on what they'll be doing later on this evening, she thought acidly. They should keep that sort of thing for the bedroom. She shut the door firmly before her mind could start inventing images of them in bed and picked up her book, struggling to get past the one sentence which she re-read three times before giving up totally. She stuck the book over her eyes and tried to take no notice of Sophia's girlish laughter and Conrad's deeper chuckles.

They might be marrying for all the convenient reasons, but it was clear to Emma that there was no shortage of physical attraction between them.

She rarely thought about men and marriage, but for the first time she felt a sharp twang inside as she contemplated what she had missed out on.

True there had been men in her life, but none that aroused more than friendship. Certainly none that had ever tempted her virginity. In fact, when it came to sex, she could never imagine what all the fuss was about.

Still, a virgin at twenty-four! What an anachronism in the twentieth century!

She turned over on to her stomach. The sun was blisteringly hot and she felt like a piece of bread in a toaster, slowly being burnt. Water, water everywhere, she thought, and not a drop to swim in, because the last thing she wanted to do was jump into the pool and disturb whatever was going on.

She didn't have to look to know that Conrad was probably enjoying Sophia's company in more ways than one.

He had struck Emma as someone who worked hard, but who also played hard. The very last thing she needed to see was him playing hard with Sophia.

Alistair's wrong, she thought, Sophia is the ideal mate for a man like Conrad. He needed someone who didn't stretch his mind. His mind was stretched enough in his work.

She heard the splashing noises as they both emerged from the pool and remained rooted in her position with her back to them. It was rude, she knew, but something inside her had twisted with a feeling of sick pain when she had seen Conrad kiss Sophia's neck. Why on earth did her emotions keep failing her, when her head still remained screwed on and was telling her that she should be careful of Conrad DeVere in more ways than one?

When Sophia sat on the lounger next to her, Emma turned around, screwing her eyes against the sun.

'We thought you might like to come to a party at my folks' house tomorrow,' she said. Conrad's hand was resting on her shoulder, and Sophia touched it with her own.

It was a careless, intimate gesture which Emma deliberately ignored.

'It's a lunch party. There'll be tennis.'

'Tennis? I have to warn you that tennis isn't one of my strong points. It's been years since I held a racket, and even then what I did with it wouldn't have got me a place at Wimbledon.'

Sophia looked blankly at her, but out of the corner of her eye Emma could see an amused smile playing on Conrad's lips.

'You mean you can't play?'

'You hit the nail on the head.'

'Oh, that's no problem.' Sophia waved aside her objection with a flippant gesture, 'I'm pretty hopeless as well. Actually, I only ever play tennis for the exercise. I have to watch my shape——' she pouted, raising her face to Conrad '—or no one else will.'

Emma smiled politely and agreed to go.

She was curious to see who would be at this tennis party. She had been sightseeing briefly a couple of times, but on her own. She was beginning to miss the company of her friends, whose letters had been erratic but full of news about places and people who seemed a lifetime away.

She also managed to buy English newspapers once a week, which were at least one week out of date, but nevertheless fun to read. She sometimes read bits aloud to Alistair, and they discussed what was happening in England with the fervour of people isolated miles away from their native land. Alistair, though he had lived in Tobago longer than he cared to remember, and though it would never have occurred to him to leave it, still felt the need to know what was going on in London.

Maybe there would be Londoners at the party.

At any rate, from what Sophia had said, there would be enough people there for Emma to more or less lose herself in the crowd.

She was beginning to feel disproportionately tense in Conrad's presence. It would do her good to meet some other people and to readjust her emotional balance.

And of course, who knew? There might be someone there who would tell her a little bit more about Alistair.

CHAPTER FOUR

IT WAS late in the morning before Emma was finally dressed, made-up, and, she felt, trussed like a chicken for the party. Two hours late. Not bad going, she thought. She quickly scanned her reflection in the long mirror, wondering if her stretchy flowered dress was really suitable for a tennis party. It would have to do. Her wardrobe wasn't exactly crammed with tiny white skirts and matching tops. In fact, her only white pair of shorts was in the wash, and Emma had no intention of rinsing them especially for the occasion.

She tiptoed towards Alistair's bedroom and peered in. Asleep. Emma frowned as she looked at him. He was supposed to be accompanying her to the party, but at the very last moment had cried off ill.

'Nothing to worry about, my dear,' he had said, when Emma had begun fussing worriedly over him. 'And stop clucking like a mother hen. Anyone would think that...'

'That...?'

'That I'd never been ill before.'

'You never take to your bed if you don't have to,' she had said anxiously.

She had, in fact, been in two minds as to whether she ought to leave him, but the combined forces of Esther and Alistair had forestalled any last-minute cancellations on her part.

Her protests that it would be no bother to give it a miss had met with Alistair's dismissive wave of the hand, and a few mumbled words about never being one to spoil other people's fun.

Nevertheless as the chauffeur dropped Emma off at the villa she still felt a twinge of uneasiness.

In the space of a few weeks she had become more than a bit fond of the old man. In the privacy of her thoughts, she considered him her grandfather. He was her own flesh and blood. The thought that he might really be ill was surprisingly painful.

She tried to put her worries aside as she was ushered into the villa. The party was in full flow. She couldn't spot either Conrad or Sophia anywhere, and she absent-mindedly accepted a glass of fruit punch, liberally laced with rum.

Sophia's parents were a striking couple. They had lived in Tobago all their lives, as had their parents, and they couldn't understand why anyone would want to live anywhere else.

'England could certainly do with a sprucing up as far as the weather is concerned.' Emma laughed. 'I get letters from my friends and they always open with the words "it hasn't stopped raining for the past week". I miss London, though, even if it is grey most of the time.'

Sophia's mother tried to look sympathetic, but clearly found it difficult.

She took her elbow and shepherded her through the guests, introducing her, explaining Alistair's absence to his acquaintances with expressions of sympathy.

'The young people are outside.' She drew Emma through the open patio doors into the sprawling garden where a mixed doubles match was in full flow, watched by clusters of guests who were applauding with what seemed like much more exuberance than the game warranted.

The demon drink, Emma thought with a grin—doesn't it loosen up everyone? She gulped the remnants of her punch and took another glass from the bar, determined to make it last more or less until it was time for her to leave. She did not drink much as a rule, and she had no intention of starting now.

Conrad was playing with Sophia. Emma watched openly as he tossed the ball into the air and sent it spinning across the net to his opponents.

His well-tuned body was embarrassingly mesmerising and she felt her eyes dwelling on his movements with painful intensity.

He and Sophia won in straight sets, which met with wild applause. As he saluted his enthusiastic spectators with mock solemnity, his eyes caught Emma's and she carelessly raised her glass to him.

'You took your time getting here,' he said as he approached her, tossing his tennis racket on a chair. The perspiration was still damp on his face and he wiped it with the back of his hand. 'I see you dressed for the occasion.'

'It was the best I could do.'

She flushed as the smile left his lips and he looked at her through dark-fringed eyes.

'Where's Alistair?' he asked abruptly.

'He wasn't feeling too good so he took a raincheck.'

'Did he get in touch with his doctor?' The sharpness in his voice startled Emma.

'No, he didn't,' she said, confused. 'Should he have? He said that it was nothing to worry about, that he'd be fine if he took his tablets and went to bed.'

The uneasy feeling was back with her. Should she have insisted that he call Doctor Tompkins? She was tempted to phone him and find out whether everything was all right.

'I'll see him when I get back,' Conrad was saying. 'If I'm in the least bit doubtful, I'll get in touch with the doctor. Alistair has a habit of sweeping aside anything to do with his health, unless he thinks it's absolutely necessary.'

Maybe it was the authoritarian tone of his voice, but Emma immediately felt herself relax. He might have his objectionable traits, but she knew implicitly that he could be relied upon. If they constantly rubbed each other up the wrong way, then that was an unavoidable personality clash and did not detract from his in-built self-assurance.

'I see your tennis match was a walkover for you,' she remarked, realising that the one and a half drinks she had had were already beginning to have their effect. 'Is there anything that you can't do?' The question was uttered with a reckless disregard for its interpretation.

'You haven't seen the best of my accomplishments,' he murmured softly, the blue eyes gleaming with irony.

Emma knew that he was teasing her but it didn't make her feel any the less confused. Amazing how he could stir her emotions with a single sentence.

'Do you normally flirt with women, even though you're engaged?'

Conrad's lips tightened.

'Even with women you don't approve of?' she persisted.

'You flatter yourself if you think I'm flirting with you,' he muttered harshly, 'I call it trying to get a reaction.'

'What would your fiancée say?'

'You could always ask her and find out.' He gave her a mocking glance and Emma's fists clenched at her side. She summoned together her fast evaporating good humour and smiled at him.

'I can think of better things to discuss.'

Sophia was approaching, having changed out of her tennis outfit into a slinky gold trouser-suit, the bottom half of which looked as though it had been painted on to her body. The top was a mere strip of stretchy material that left little to the imagination.

She resembled some wild jungle animal, perhaps a puma, with her glowing bronzed skin and golden cat-like eyes. She linked her arm through Conrad's and Emma was struck at how physically well matched they were. There was something predatory about Conrad as well, but, in his case, latently dangerous.

Sophia looked at them and smiled, her yellow-gold eyes flickering invitingly over Conrad. 'Enjoying yourself?' she asked Emma.

'She's having a great time.' Conrad looked at her, one eyebrow raised in amusement, and Emma felt a strong urge to tip her drink over his head.

'I'll leave you to continue enjoying yourself without me.' He sauntered off and Sophia turned to Emma, chatting politely about the various people at the party, most of whom she had come into contact with in her line of work, one way or another.

All the while, her eyes skimmed the crowd, acknowledging the appreciative glances of some of the men with pouting approval.

She was like a flower, some rare and beautiful species which only blossomed in the company of men. They were her sun and water. It amused Emma to see that, although she talked to her, it was absent-mindedly, as though she was merely passing the time of day until something more exciting beckoned.

'I should really be on a shoot in Istanbul,' she explained in a low voice to Emma, 'but Conrad insisted that I come over here for a while. He never usually insists on my dropping my work to be with him, so I decided to come over. Anyway, at the last minute I managed to persuade the photographer, who's a friend of mine, to switch the shoot from Istanbul to here, hence this crowd.' She gesticulated broadly at the milling crowd and sipped from her glass.

Emma had stopped listening. Her thoughts were whirring in another direction.

So Conrad had insisted that Sophia fly to Tobago to be with him. What was it he had said about not believing in love? Obviously he couldn't bear to be apart from Sophia for too long. And you thought he was flirting with you, she reproved herself. The idea made her blush with shame.

Wishful thinking, she told herself, with punishing accuracy. True, there was something in his personality which made her feel defensive and angry, but why deny that he was a physically attractive man? He made no effort to deny it, for heaven's sake! He was fully aware of the effect that he had on women.

An alarming thought crossed her mind. What if he was aware of the effect he had on her? Emma shuddered.

She restlessly listened to Sophia's chatter, twirling her glass in her hand and inwardly cringing at what a fool she risked making of herself.

For starters, she was not his type any more than he was hers. Looking at it from that perspective was more to her liking and she dwelt on all the facets of his personality that she found disagreeable. His arrogance, his easy charm, that thread of ruthlessness which was sensed rather than seen.

Yes, he was not her type at all.

Anyway, he was the last person she should be attracted to anyway. He was engaged, for starters. Emma had always made a point of avoiding married men. An engaged man was more or less of the same ilk.

Besides, he had made his position quite clear on gold-diggers. She did not by any means fall into that category, but what if he were to find out about her connection with Alistair? Wouldn't he see her as the long-lost granddaughter who had travelled halfway across the world at the first possible opportunity, just to see what she could get out of an old, but extremely rich man?

True, he would find out in due course, but she had no intention of being around when he did.

So, she thought, reasons to avoid him.

She was feeling quite pleased with herself when Sophia gestured towards a tall, fair-haired man whom she proudly introduced as her brother.

'I got all the looks,' he joked. 'As you can see, Sophia's only passable in comparison.'

He had the healthy, tanned look of a beachcomber, and Emma was surprised when he announced that he actually lived in Trinidad and ran a nightclub. She accepted another glass of punch and listened to him as he told her about what was involved in running a club. He was clearly enamoured of life in the tropics, had no intention of ever leaving, and good-humouredly tried to persuade her that England was no comparison to an island where even the rainfall was warm.

Emma found herself laughing in response to him, liking his easy manner. He was much more like the sort of men she was accustomed to dating. He didn't rouse her and he was no challenge. She could relax with him, speak to him on friendly terms. Most of all, he did not threaten her self-control. She smiled as he began describing the girl he was going out with and who had had to remain in Trinidad for the weekend because of work.

'What do you think of your sister's jet-setting,' she teased, 'if you're so adamant that there's no life beside island life? Don't you think that she might fall in love with Europe?'

'Youth,' he said airily, even though Emma suspected that he could not be more than twenty-five, 'will travel. Mind you, she'll be settling down soon enough when she marries Conrad.'

Emma nodded non-committally.

'Not,' he added, 'that she's too keen on the idea, although she assures me that she wants to have babies, and the sooner, the better. Fact is, though, she's only just twenty and she can't see herself in a mansion with only herself for company. Modelling's spoilt her somewhat. All that action. You know.'

Emma replied that she didn't really have a clue.

'Still,' he sighed, 'wedded bliss. It's got to happen some time. My number'll be up before I know it.'

She laughed sympathetically and, when he slipped his arm around her waist to walk with her to the bar, she relaxed against him.

A clipped, icy voice behind her made her swing around. Conrad was staring at her, his eyes cool and disdainful.

'Hope I'm not breaking anything up,' he said with no hint of apology in his voice. His hand snaked out, grasping her by the wrist and forcing her to face him. 'I've been looking for you,' he told her brusquely.

'What for? I'm managing perfectly well on my own!'

'So I see,' he muttered sarcastically. 'Do you normally find it so easy to mix with the crowd?'

'Yes!' Emma bit out angrily, yanking her hand away. 'Especially when "the crowd" happens to be someone as pleasant as Lloyd!'

'Well said, darling.' Lloyd grinned at her and winked. Out of sheer perversity she winked back, disregarding Conrad's thunderous look.

'Lighten up, Conrad.' Lloyd draped his arm around her neck and grinned disarmingly. 'Emma's not spoken for.'

Conrad ignored his remark. He looked at Emma and said, 'You. Follow me.' Then he turned away and began walking towards the house. Emma quickly and apologetically disengaged herself from Lloyd's stranglehold and followed Conrad's rapidly retreating back.

When she finally caught up with him, she rounded on him furiously. 'Just who do you think you are, dragging me away from a conversation like some kind of prisoner under arrest? Issuing orders for me to follow you, no less! If you want to throw your weight around, then I suggest you go do it with Sophia!'

'Call me your Guardian Angel,' he bit out, barely controlling his anger, 'I'm saving you from Lloyd, whose womanising reputation precedes him by several miles. From what I saw of him draped all over you, you were next on his list of conquests.'

'Well, thank you very much!' Emma said coldly, enunciating each word carefully. 'I can take care of myself, if it's all the same to you!'

She had no intention of telling him that the womanising Lloyd had in fact spent the last twenty minutes telling her about his girlfriend.

'Anyway, I'm not here to argue with you,' he told her tightly, 'I've just had a call from Esther. Alistair's taken a turn for the worse. She's calling the doctor. I'm going there now. I thought,' he added, emphasising the word, 'that you might like to come along with me, but if you're otherwise occupied . . .?'

'I'll get my bag,' Emma told him quickly, throwing over her shoulder as she walked away. 'You might have said that from the start, instead of beating about the bush. I'll meet you at the car in five minutes.'

She hastily apologised to Sophia's parents for her late arrival and early exit, nodding in frustration as they invited her to come again any time.

Her mind was racing ahead, praying that Alistair was all right and that it was all a false alarm. She knew that he was not well, but had never asked exactly how unwell he was. He had always been so alert with her that she'd never imagined it could be anything serious.

She, of all people, should have known that to rely on someone being alive indefinitely was to rely on an illusion. Hadn't her mother survived the car crash, told by doctors that she would be all right, only to die two weeks later?

Conrad was waiting by the car, his long fingers drumming impatiently on the bonnet. When he spotted her running towards him, he stepped into the driver's seat, reaching out to fling open the passenger door.

'What exactly did Esther say?' Emma wanted to know, as the engine throbbed into life and he carefully manoeuvred the car out of the drive. 'Did she give you any details? I mean, is it a heart attack?'

'She just said to come quickly. He's collapsed. She's put him to bed and he seemed to be getting his colour back, but...'

Conrad let the sentence hang in the air and Emma bit worriedly on her lip. But... That implied all sorts of things, and none of them pleasant.

And she hadn't even told him about her mother, about her relationship to him. She should have. She should have told him from the start instead of settling on some damn fool idea of keeping it to herself until she got to know him better.

Now she could only hope that it was not going to be too late.

'Hurry up,' she urged Conrad, only to be told that narrow, twisting roads did not encourage speed.

'Relax,' he told her grimly, 'And for God's sake put your seatbelt on.'

Emma obeyed without thinking.

She settled back against the seat, absent-mindedly watching the landscape roll past. Coconut trees, glimpses of some of the bluest sea she had ever seen, white sand shimmering under the heat.

'Don't think the worst,' Conrad said with maddening self-control. He placed his hand on her leg and Emma felt the warmth of his hand singe her flesh like fire. She flinched away and he immediately withdrew his hand.

'Sorry,' he drawled. 'Forgot. You're a lady who doesn't like too much physical contact. Not even, it would appear, contact of the innocent kind. You prefer Lloyd's brand of highly suspect fondling.'

'I never said that!' Emma protested angrily. 'And Lloyd's so-called "fondling" was not "highly suspect".'

She looked at him covertly, her eyes taking in his strong, tanned arms, the fine black hair curling around his watch-strap, the uncompromising lines of his face.

'As you like. Although I'm amazed you let him touch you. From the way that you recoil every time I accidentally brush against you, I would have thought that contact of any kind was to be avoided.'

Emma was stung by his assumption. 'Just because I'm not attracted to you, it doesn't mean I'm afraid of physical contact.' She lifted her chin defiantly. Conrad's eyes flicked away from the road for an instant, resting on her full lips.

Emma looked away in confusion. Wasn't it a good thing that he thought her some kind of ice maiden? If she had any sense at all, she would work on cultivating the image instead of seeing it as an accusation. Ice maidens didn't react to men like Conrad. She would do well to remember that.

'Is Lloyd more your type of man?' Conrad asked in a tone of mild interest.

He had slowed the car down to compensate for the narrowing of the roads. Every so often, he would have to swerve slightly to avoid ruts in the tarmac.

Emma's stomach tightened at his question. The air-conditioning in the car had been switched on, but she felt suddenly hot. She rolled down the window fractionally, but, feeling the blast of hot air, she immediately rolled it back up.

'I don't have a type,' she replied stiffly, folding her arms across her chest. She could feel her breasts hard under the soft fall of her dress, the nipples pressing against the thin material.

She had a wild yearning desire for him to reach out and touch her. Her fingers tightened on the bare flesh of her arms, leaving red indentations.

'No,' Conrad agreed softly. At that moment he swerved to avoid a deep rut, sending the car jolting to one side. Emma's arm banged against the car door and she yelped.

'Are you all right?' Conrad asked, slowing the car to a standstill, but keeping the engine running.

'I can see why you insist on seatbelts.' Emma rubbed her arm and examined it.

'Let me have a look.'

'No!' she snapped, watching with consternation as he unfastened himself and stretched across her. She forced herself to appear calm. 'It's fine. Let's just get going and get this journey done with. Please. I want to see how Alistair is, and the sooner we get there, the better.'

Conrad shrugged and turned away. 'Suit yourself, but I'd rather not have two invalids on my hands.'

As the car pulled slowly away, Emma relaxed against the cushioned headrest and breathed a sigh of relief.

She closed her eyes and relinquished herself to the swaying of the car. She had over-reacted again, she realised. She had spent years erecting invisible barriers between herself and the opposite sex, only to discover that when she most needed them they were lying crumbled at her feet.

When she next opened her eyes the car was swinging into the drive to Alistair's house.

Emma sat up abruptly. All her previous anxiety had resettled like a knot in the pit of her stomach. Before the car had stopped, she was fumbling with the door-handle and unfastening her seatbelt.

She ran up to the front door and let herself in, aware that Conrad was following behind her but at a more leisurely pace.

'Where is he?' she asked Esther, who had appeared from the kitchen.

'Upstairs, with the doctor.'

Emma turned to Conrad. 'What shall we do? Do you think we ought to go up and see what's happening?'

'I think we can rely on Doctor Tompkins to emerge in due course and tell us what's happening,' he replied drily. 'There are no ambulances and he hasn't been taken to hospital, so I think we can assume that he's in a stable condition.'

'You're so practical!'

'Well, one of us has to be.' He smiled at her and his face was transformed.

'You should smile more often,' she said impulsively.

His smile broadened to a grin. 'I do. Quite often. You just spend so much time arguing with me that you don't get to see it.'

'Me?' Emma's green eyes looked at him incredulously, 'I never argue with you! It's always the other way around!'

'There you go again.'

She felt a sudden surge of warmth towards him. She knew instinctively what he was trying to do with his light-hearted bantering. He was trying to relieve some of her tension, to relax her, and it was working.

She heard Doctor Tompkins descending the staircase and raised her eyes to him with a sense of dread.

'Is he going to be all right?' Conrad strode towards the doctor, looking strangely incongruous in his shorts and T-shirt next to the doctor, who was more formally dressed, and carrying his black bag.

Doctor Tompkins was thin and dark, his curly hair almost completely grey, with a crisp, efficient manner. He looked reticently towards Emma, as if asking himself whether he should recognise her.

'She works for Alistair,' Conrad informed him in a clipped voice, correctly interpreting the question mark in his eyes. 'You can speak freely in front of her.'

The doctor nodded and said in a precise, professional tone that Alistair had expressed a desire not to have him discuss his condition with either Conrad or Emma.

Conrad looked at the doctor in surprise. 'Why not?'

Doctor Tompkins shrugged and looked at his watch. 'I'm running late for another appointment.' He glanced at them and his face softened. 'I've given Mr Jackson a prescription. Two tablets to be taken three times a day. He's to take it easy. Rest, relaxation and no drink whatsoever, not even a smell of whisky.'

'But he's going to be fine,' Emma interjected. 'Isn't he?'

'He wants to explain it to you himself. 'I really don't know why, but, as you are well aware, I'm duty-bound to adhere to a patient's wishes.'

Conrad nodded in silence.

'I'll be back in a couple of days' time to check him over.'

They both watched as the doctor shut the front door firmly behind him, and turned to each other. Coming hard on the heels of her anxiety of a few moments before, Emma had a feeling of bewildered let-down. What did the doctor mean that Alistair wanted to talk about his condition to them himself?

When they entered his room, it was to find the old man propped up in his bed, his face pale and subdued.

He looked at them both and gestured to Emma to sit next to him.

'I'm an old man,' he began pathetically. He looked at his hands and shook his head.

'What did the doctor say?' Conrad asked, breaking into what looked like a budding monologue on old age. He had his emotions under a tight rein, but even so Emma could detect in him the same worry that she was feeling.

Only, she guessed, he would not be the sort to rant and rave and tear at his hair. That strong, self-imposed discipline of his was too ingrained in his personality to ever give way like that.

'I'm to rest,' Alistair told them in a low voice. He turned to Emma and informed her sadly that he was not the man he used to be.

With an impulsive gesture, she reached out and slipped her hand into his. She looked up at Conrad and met cool, icy eyes.

'You still haven't told us what the doctor said, apart from that you need to rest. Which, incidentally, is what he's been saying for the last five years.'

Conrad approached the bed, his hands in his shorts pockets. 'What did the doctor say?'

'I'm sorry I dragged you both away from your party.'

'Never mind about the party,' Emma murmured reassuringly, receiving an affectionate pat on the hand.

Alistair sighed deeply, and was it her imagination or could she see tears pricking at the back of his eyes? She felt her heart constrict. All those feelings that had assailed her in the wake of her mother's death were with her again, and there was regret too. She had known Alistair for so short a time, too short.

She had still not recovered from the death of her mother. She still felt the loss that came when someone whose presence had been around from time beginning suddenly was no longer there. She did not want to think of the pain of having to endure a second loss.

'He doesn't know how much longer I've got,' Alistair said heavily. He pressed his fingers to his eyes as though wanting to shut out the seriousness of his words.

Emma gasped in shock. She had been expecting the worst, and now that it had been confirmed an icy chill settled on her.

Conrad was looking at him, his face controlled, his expression unreadable. He sat on the side of the bed, opposite Emma, his vivid eyes resting on Alistair's face.

'Is there anything we can get for you?' he asked roughly.

'My children.' Alistair either didn't hear or else chose to ignore Conrad's question. 'I've spent a long time acquiring wealth, and at the end of the day I'm not sure if I've managed to acquire happiness. There are a lot of things in life that I regret doing, and even more I regret not having done. Now I'm an old man with not much longer left to live. I want to speak my mind.'

He turned to Conrad, 'You might tell me that it's none of my business, but you really musn't marry Sophia. She's too young, and too...' He searched for the right word. 'Too stupid for you. I know it's convenient and that you've known her off and on for a long time, but that doesn't make it right. I guess I'm the last person in the world to offer advice about marriage, but you can forgive the frankness of an old, dying man.'

'I know how you feel about this engagement, Alistair,' Conrad said, with a touch of impatience in his voice. 'You've spoken to me about it frequently enough. What we want to find out is exactly what the doctor said to you.'

Alistair ignored him. 'It would be different if you were madly in love with her, but this plan of yours to commit yourself for life to someone merely because it happens to be convenient... Well, it can only end in tears.'

Conrad was wearing the caged, helpless look of someone who wanted to argue a point, and was resisting through sheer will-power.

He ran his fingers frustratedly through his black hair and frowned heavily. 'We've been through this a thousand times, Alistair, from every conceivable angle, and...'

'It would, of course, be my dying wish,' Alistair treated Conrad's interjection with admirable nonchalance, 'to see you married, but to the right girl. Someone with energy and a mind of her own. Someone who could relate to you on an equal basis.' He glanced at Emma and smiled, absent-mindedly patting her hand.

Oh, no, she thought; oh, no. Matchmaking? He had just finished informing them that he was old and ill, and yet he still could find time for matchmaking?

A hundred little things suddenly slotted into place, like pieces of a jigsaw puzzle. She was torn between an aching compassion for Alistair—a sick man after all—and a strong desire to inform him that there was no way that Conrad was going to find someone with energy and a mind of her own, if that someone just happened to be her. They only just managed to tolerate each other, for heaven's sake! Besides, Emma was convinced that men did not suddenly change their tastes in women. They were drawn to variations of the same type, either physically or intellectually. And she had seen ample proof of the sort of women Conrad preferred.

For that matter, he was hardly to her liking.

She sat upright.

'I think we should leave you to rest now.' Conrad's words managed to rescue the silence which had threatened to become embarrassingly prolonged. 'There's no point in overtiring yourself, that much the doctor did impart,' he added pointedly.

'Yes, perhaps you're right.' Alistair shut his eyes and sank lower into the bedclothes. 'Could you send Esther up with some lunch for me?' he asked in a weak, tired voice. 'A poached egg and some salmon, and perhaps just a piece of some of that coconut sweetbread she made yesterday. Also a cup of sweet tea and a slice of her ginger cake.'

'Salmon? Coconut sweetbread? Ginger cake, for heaven's sake? Should you be eating that sort of stuff?' Conrad stood up and looked down at Alistair through narrowed eyes.

'The doctor told me to rest, not to starve.'

'We understand,' Emma said hurriedly. She frowned warningly at Conrad. 'I'll send her up with a tray in a moment. But first, I'd like to talk with you. Alone. If you're not too tired.'

She could sense that watchful air settle on Conrad like an invisible cloud.

'What's it in connection with?' he asked, staring at her, trying to read her mind.

'None of your business.'

'Alistair's ill,' Conrad said smoothly, 'I have to know whether what you have to say is going to upset him. He's supposed to rest, don't forget.'

You devious swine, Emma thought, playing on the situation for what it was worth. Typical.

'Will you two stop talking over my head as though I weren't here?' Alistair spoke, with a return to his former self. 'Go away, Conrad. I'll be fine.'

Emma grinned triumphantly at Conrad and met with a frowning response. Checkmate, she thought.

He walked towards the door, and stood there for a few seconds, staring at her as though he was trying to read her mind.

'Goodbye,' she said meaningfully, and was rewarded with a thunderous glare. He grunted something which she didn't catch, and shut the door gently. Emma turned to Alistair.

'There's something I think you should know,' she began hesitantly. 'I've been putting off this moment, but the time has come for me to tell you.'

CHAPTER FIVE

ALISTAIR looked at her with interest. All traces of illness seemed to have vanished and his colour had returned.

Emma twisted her hands nervously together on her lap. How to proceed from here? She had fleetingly considered this moment in the past few weeks, but she had had no idea that when it finally arrived it would find her so helpless.

'There's something I must go and get,' she eventually murmured. 'I won't be long.'

'I'll wait here,' Alistair promised. 'There's nowhere I can go.'

He was true to his word. When Emma returned, he seemed hardly to have shifted position. Without a word, she handed him the letter which she was carrying in her hand. Her mother had written it after the accident, even though she had been told by her doctor that she was on the road to recovery. Perhaps she had had forebodings of her own death.

'Give this to your grandfather,' she had instructed Emma. 'Even if you decide never to see him, make sure that he gets this. It's so late, too late now for me, but I must make my peace somehow.'

Emma had not known what was in the letter, and she still did not know.

As Alistair slit open the envelope and began to read, the room became so still that Emma could hear all the noises outside, the sound of the distant sea, the soft breeze stirring the grass and trees into rustling movement, almost as though magnified.

She waited patiently until Alistair had finished, not saying a word when he looked at her and then back to the letter, which he re-read three times.

'So,' he said.

There was a heavy silence. Alistair seemed wrapped up in his thoughts, and Emma did not want to disturb them.

Conflicting emotions surged through her. Painful memories of her mother, anxiety that her revelation might be such a shock to Alistair that he might suffer a relapse, relief that what she had come to do was finally done.

She studied Alistair's face carefully, pleased to see that he seemed to be handling the news well.

He folded the letter, stuck it into his top pocket and folded his hands on the blanket.

'I wondered when you would tell me,' he said gently.

'I wanted to find out about you for myself,' Emma began awkwardly, 'I needed to put everything in perspective. Only you fell ill...and then I was so worried that...' She stopped and shot him a surprised look. 'What do you mean, you wondered when I would tell you...?'

'I knew who you were, my dear, from the very first moment you walked through the front door.' He smiled delightedly at her confusion.

'You knew?' Emma's mouth dropped open in amazement. She didn't know whether to laugh, to cry, or to be angry. 'How?' she asked in astonishment. She sat on the edge of the bed.

'Well, my dear, believe it or not, I managed to trace your mother quite soon after she left Tobago with that man. But she refused to have anything to do with me, and after a while I thought it best to leave her alone until she had worked out her problems. But she never did.' He sighed, gesturing to Emma to pass him the box of tissues. 'I knew of her pregnancy, and of your existence, and I waited and hoped . . . What else could I do? Maybe more. I don't know. Maybe I should have forced a reconciliation.'

Emma shook her head dumbly, at a loss for words.

'I continued to keep tabs on her over the years, so that at least I could reassure myself that she was all right. When she died, a little of me died as well. But then you came along, like a breath of fresh air into my life. When you arrived here and didn't breathe a word of who you really were, I suspected that you wanted to find out about me in your own time, make up your own mind, and I respected that.'

'You naughty old man.' Emma smiled slowly. 'What must you have thought of me?'

'I loved you.' He patted her hand and pulled her towards him affectionately. 'Of course, now that it's out in the open, it'll be all the better, because I can call you granddaughter. I've been dying to call you that since you arrived.'

Emma laughed, feeling a rush of elation flood through her. 'You're crafty,' she accused him warmly.

'Well, craftier than you, little one.'

There was a sharp rap on the door, and they both jumped as Conrad walked into the room. He had changed out of his tennis shorts and T-shirt into a pair of faded jeans and a pale blue shirt. His eyes swept over them, resting quizzically on Emma.

'Have I interrupted something . . .?' he asked in a hard voice.

'As a matter of fact, you have, son,' Alistair replied, 'something wonderful.'

Emma looked in panic at Alistair. 'I don't think . . .'

Alistair was looking above her head to Conrad, and either genuinely didn't see or else chose not to see her mouthing the words, 'not now.'

'I'd like to introduce you to Emma Belle, my granddaughter.'

From behind her, Emma could feel Conrad's eyes on her, the coiled tension of his body, as he moved smoothly to the other side of the bed.

'Well, well, well,' he said softly, forcing her to meet his eyes. 'So this was your little secret.'

Alistair was looking at both of them, his eyes darting from one face to the other.

'Oh, dear,' he cut in, 'I feel quite weak all of a sudden. It must be the shock. Emma, dear, do pass me that cup of water on the table.'

She reached out for it, casually peering inside, and then suspiciously sniffing the contents. 'There's whisky in here!'

'Is there?' Alistair asked innocently. 'Oh, dear. Well, that'll just have to do, then.'

He plucked the cup out of her hands and swallowed a mouthful of the amber liquid, then lay back on the bed with his eyes shut. 'Much better. Even so, I do feel rather tired,' he murmured weakly. 'Perhaps you could leave me alone for a moment...?'

'Sure.' Conrad stood up and removed the cup from his hands. 'Get some sleep, Alistair, and no drink. Remember the doctor's orders.'

'Pah!'

'I'll see you later, Grandfather.' She kissed him on the forehead, ignoring his plea for just one more sip of the whisky before he settled down to sleep.

She knew that Conrad was staring at her, and she defiantly refused to meet the hard, questioning glint in his eyes.

She told herself firmly that she didn't give a damn what he thought of her now. Why on earth should she? He had thought the worst of her from the very beginning, and if this only served to cement his opinion of her, then so be it.

Conrad didn't say a word to her as they stepped out into the corridor, quietly shutting the bedroom door behind them. He turned away and walked quickly down the staircase, and Emma followed reluctantly.

She could just as easily have gone to her bedroom, in fact to any other room in the house which happened to be in the opposite direction to where Conrad was walking, but for some reason her feet refused to comply with reason. She found herself running behind him, until they were both in the sitting-room, and he had shut the door behind them.

Then he turned to face her. She watched the implacable set of his features with first dismay, and then anger. She didn't owe him an explanation, for heaven's sake! She wasn't going to let him intimidate her into thinking that she had somehow done something wrong!

'So you're the little granddaughter come home to roost,' he drawled, toying with one of the ornamental figurines which had been resting on the table, his long fingers twirling it around absent-mindedly.

'I'm Alistair's granddaughter, yes! Not that it has anything to do with you.'

His fingers tightened on the tiny statuette, and she watched in fascination, wondering whether he would snap it in two, but he replaced it on the table and stuck his hands in his pockets.

'As I told you before, everything you do is my business. Why did you come here? Why now?'

The blue eyes were cold and vaguely threatening.

'If you must know,' Emma said icily, 'it was the first opportunity I got after my mother's death. I couldn't come sooner, because Mum wouldn't have wanted me to.'

'She said so?'

'Not in so many words, no! I refuse to be put through this . . .'

She turned to walk away, and felt his hand clamp around her arm.

'Not so fast.'

'Let me go!' Emma wriggled uselessly against him, her rapid breathing making her breasts rise and fall quickly.

'How do I know that you haven't decided to come over here, suddenly full of granddaughterly love, because you know that Alistair is rich and his caring handouts could be very valuable to you?'

'You don't! But, just for the record, I haven't!'

His grip slackened, and she faced him, her mouth going dry as their eyes met. His head dipped down, and before she could pull away she felt his lips on her, savagely forcing open her mouth until his tongue was inside, probing her. A giddy excitement swept through her body, and her hands clenched his shirt convulsively as she returned his kiss, unable to fight the sudden, reckless yearning filling her.

This was madness. Part of her mind was screaming for her to stop, but the feverish pleasure she felt was so powerful. She could hardly catch her breath under the force of his kiss. How could she listen to reason?

He drew back with a lazy smile. 'Well, at least I know now that you won't be another Lisa St Clair.'

Emma looked at the devilish, dangerous face and ran out of the room, slamming the door behind her.

Her body was burning when she finally made it to her room and leaned against the door with her eyes shut. What had she been thinking when she'd let him kiss her? He didn't even like her, but even so he had managed to stir feelings in her that had risen from their slumbering depths like alarming, uncontrollable monsters.

Where had her common sense been when she had needed it? She breathed slowly, gradually feeling her body relax.

She had made a mistake. But mistakes could be rectified, and experiences, even incomprehensible ones, could be lessons. This one certainly would be.

When she descended the staircase next morning, she felt totally in control.

Conrad was in the kitchen, and he looked up as she came in.

His eyes flickered unhurriedly over her and Emma ignored him.

'Is this the ice maiden act?' he mocked.

'Has Esther made this bread for lunch?'

'Yes. Why don't you look me in the face when you're talking to me?'

'Because,' Emma said blandly, 'there's a host of other things I would rather look at. How's Sophia?'

'Ah! Reminding me that engaged men don't kiss other women, right?'

Emma flushed. That had been precisely her point, not that it seemed to have thrown him at all.

'She's fine. Actually, we'll be going to the beach after lunch. Pigeon Point. Would the ice maiden like to come along with us?'

'No.'

'Why not?'

'I have other things to do.' She bit into her sandwich and threw him a glacial stare.

'Like what?' Conrad leaned back in the chair and looked at her with a trace of amusement. 'Washing your hair? Painting your nails? It surely can't be work, because at the moment, without Alistair, you're a bit superfluous around here. I take it that you do intend to continue working, that your job here wasn't entirely a hoax to get into the family mansion?'

'You take it right!' Emma said, her pretence at calm giving way to anger.

'Then you'll be a bit bored here for a while. Alistair won't be back on his feet for at least a week, if not longer. So, come along to the beach with us.'

'A threesome?' Emma could have kicked herself for saying it, but it had been the first thing that had sprang to mind. Conrad, Sophia and . . . her.

'Does that bother you?' Conrad was looking at her intently and Emma felt the colour rise to her cheeks.

'No, of course not,' Emma said defensively. 'I just wouldn't want to get in the way of . . .'

'Of what? We won't be doing anything intimate on the beach, you know.'

He stared at her and laughed.

'I do think I've embarrassed you,' he said lazily, looking at her sideways.

Emma could feel her skin going a deeper shade of red and concentrated with unnecessary thoroughness on her sandwich. He was still wearing an infuriating half-smile on his face and she could quite easily have kicked him under the table.

'I'd love to come to the beach with you,' she said sweetly. 'Since I've been here, I haven't seen anything at all. Apart from the cove at the bottom of the garden.'

'Ah, yes, the cove.' He grinned and Emma regarded him with stony incomprehension. 'Pigeon Point, I have to tell you, isn't quite as private as that. But I think you'll find that the bathing more than compensates for any lack of privacy.'

He left the kitchen, whistling. I hope he gets stung by a jelly fish, Emma thought furiously.

Her nerves were still on edge when she left the house half an hour later to find both Sophia and Lloyd in the car waiting for her.

Conrad emerged from the house slightly behind her, his eyes raking over the occupants of the car.

'I didn't realise that you were coming, Lloyd,' he said in a voice which implied that if Lloyd's presence in the car was a surprise then it was an unpleasant one. 'Don't you have a nightclub to run in Trinidad? Or do you find the prospect of work in this weather a little off-putting at the moment?'

Emma stared at his cool expression in surprise. Personally, she was relieved that there was going to be a fourth person.

Lloyd smiled at her and she smiled back, disregarding Conrad's surly appraisal of them.

'We'll take the Range Rover, I think,' he said abruptly. 'There's more room.'

Without waiting for a response, he walked off towards Alistair's Range Rover, and they followed him, Lloyd with his arm around Emma's neck.

Conrad, Emma thought as she watched the angry pulse beating in his neck, was, on top of everything else, moody.

She looked from her position in the back seat at the unyielding set of his jaw, and wondered what could be eating him. He'd been fine when he had been laughing at her less than an hour before.

She decided to put all unwelcome thoughts of Conrad DeVere out of her mind, and sat back, lazily watching the scenery flash past, listening to Lloyd's chatter and laughing with ready amusement at some of his stories.

He was a social being, easy to be with, and ready with conversation to fill any potential gaps of silence.

Emma could quite easily lapse into a world of her own, and she did, thinking of Alistair and trying to ignore Sophia's proximity to Conrad in the front.

When the car slowed down and pulled up to the beach, Emma sat upright and gulped down the unbelievable picture postcard of the beach.

Of course, she had known that it would be beautiful, but she was still amazed at the turquoise clarity of the water and the feather softness of the white sands. The sea here was protected by a coral reef, which she could just see in the distance, and as a result the water was as calm as a swimming pool, the breeze barely causing it to ripple as it washed up on to the shoreline.

'Crowded,' Conrad said ruefully, pointing at another couple in the distance with two young children.

'You're kidding,' Emma remarked, gazing at the emptiness.

Sophia had run ahead and was already spreading out her towel and easing herself out of her skin-tight denim shorts and white vest. Lloyd had stripped off with slightly less aplomb and was splashing in the water, whooping with the enthusiasm of a ten-year-old.

Emma sauntered slowly with Conrad towards the patch of sand that Sophia had picked out. If I were Sophia, she thought, I would be reaching out right now to hold his hand. The idea was so silly that she speeded up and quickly slipped off her jersey top, acutely conscious that Conrad was doing the same.

What on earth does the man eat? she wondered, sneaking a sideways glance at him. There was not an ounce of fat on him; every inch seemed moulded to perfection. He lay down alongside Sophia, his head resting on his arm, and pulled a peaked cloth cap over his face so that he could see what was happening on the beach without being over-exposed to the sun.

'I can't stay too long in this heat,' Sophia observed, turning to face Emma. 'Can't risk any sunburn at all. Model's nightmare.' She yawned and Emma thought that it was just as well that she wasn't in any occupation like that, because she intended to get as much sun as possible.

'No sun and no food,' Conrad commented drily. 'Is it worth it?'

'You know I have to stay in shape.' Sophia pouted. 'You wouldn't love me if I didn't.'

He raised one eyebrow, but did not comment. Say it, Emma willed, tell her that you love her, isn't that why you asked her to come over specifically to join you in Tobago?

She squinted at Lloyd, who seemed to be a mere dot in the distance, although she could see that he was still standing, with the water reaching him only slightly above the waist.

She stood up and walked slowly towards the water. It was beautifully warm. Emma paddled out to join Lloyd and immediately joined in a water fight with him, kicking away as he swam and tried to grab her legs. She lost herself in the sheer fun of it, lying on her back and floating alongside him when they had both exhausted themselves.

As they drifted to the motion of the current, she listened to him as he told her about his love-life, which, he said, was all over.

'I thought it was the real thing,' Emma commented with amusement.

'It was. At the time.'

She laughed, spluttering as he pulled her underneath the water. When she felt his lips brush against hers, she was surprised but didn't pull away.

'Is this the best you can offer to a heartbroken young man?' he asked with a grin.

'Heartbroken young men should be cooped up in a dark room, wondering how they're ever going to recover and finding relief in huge boxes of chocolates.'

'That's what heartbroken young women do,' Lloyd responded vigorously. 'We men are braver.'

'Ah.' Emma nodded sagely. 'By braver I take it you mean that you immediately find a replacement for the last girlfriend?'

This time Lloyd didn't answer. Instead, he grabbed her by the waist, and this time his kiss was harder, more demanding. His lips covered hers, and she could feel his tongue moving against hers, demanding a response.

Emma pushed him away to arm's length.

'Whoa. I don't intend to be the replacement,' she protested, but couldn't help laughing when he pulled a comic face. With Lloyd love and lovemaking was a game, one to be lost or won, but either way with the same degree of good humour.

He did not excite a response in her, but she could not find it in her heart to be severe. Besides, she had a feeling that severity was the last thing in the world that would deter Lloyd. He was too full of boyish enthusiasm to take it seriously.

His hands circled her waist and he said with an exaggerated French accent, 'We could make sweet music together.'

Emma giggled hysterically. 'With that phony French accent?'

'I have quite a large repertoire of accents. How about a Russian one?'

'No way.'

'Humphrey Bogart?'

Emma shook her head.

'I guess,' Lloyd said mournfully, 'you're telling me that we won't be making sweet music together after all.' He pretended to wipe a tear away from the side of his face. 'I'm crushed.'

'You will be in a minute if you don't stop acting the wounded animal.' She lunged at him, tickling him under his arms as he tried to escape by splashing her.

'Femme sans merci!' he yelped. 'Or whatever!'

They were still giggling as they headed back towards the beach. Lloyd threw his arm around her neck with brotherly affection.

'Look me up if you're ever in Trinidad,' he said soberly. 'I'll show you a good time, absolutely no strings attached.'

Emma promised. She would do it, as well. She liked Lloyd, and felt that they could become friends. She impulsively squeezed his hand and grinned up at him.

When she looked ahead, it was to find Conrad staring at her from underneath his cap with brooding intensity.

Sophia waved at them. She had covered herself with a large white shirt and was wearing a wide-brimmed hat to shade her face.

'I think it's time we left,' Conrad said abruptly, as Emma sat down on the towel and prepared to smother her body with suntan oil.

'Already?' Sophia looked at him in surprise. 'We've only been here an hour. I'll have a quick dip, then,' she said, reading the cool, uncompromising expression on his face.

She walked gracefully towards the water, gently splashing her body with water as she submerged.

'We should have brought two cars,' Lloyd commented. 'Emma and I could have followed on.' He turned to her. 'Don't you agree, my little chickadee?'

Emma tried to stifle her giggle and failed.

'Shame, isn't it?' Conrad said in a frozen voice. His eyes were chips of ice.

What's eating him? Emma wondered. He had not glanced at her once, but she could feel the coldness emanating from his body in a wave. Maybe he had had an argument with Sophia, although the few times that she had spotted them from the water they had not seemed to be talking, far less having an argument.

Anyway, if he had argued with her, it was downright unfair to take it out on Lloyd, who had retreated into a bewildered silence.

'Perhaps we could come back here another day?' she remarked, turning to Lloyd.

This time Conrad did look at her and his expression was flint-hard. 'Have you forgotten why you're here?' he asked coldly. 'You're here to work. So you say. It's what you're being handsomely paid for. You're not here to frolic on the beach every day so that you can improve your suntan.'

'I have no intention of frolicking on the beach every day!' Emma spluttered angrily. 'To improve my suntan!

For your information, this is about the first day I've taken off, and that's only because Alistair's ill and can't work at the moment! So don't you dare accuse me of shirking!'

She looked at him scathingly and a dark red flush crept up his face.

'I never accused you of anything,' he said harshly. 'You accused yourself. Perhaps it's a guilty conscience getting the better of you.'

Emma clenched her fists impotently at her sides.

She watched him as he strode towards the sea and muttered a few curt words to Sophia.

'You two seem to get along well,' Lloyd commented mildly.

'Does anyone get along with a cobra?'

'Oh, I don't know. Sophia tells me that all her friends find him wildly attractive and it's got nothing to do with the size of his bank balance. I think that half the thrill with Sophia is that she feels as if she's netted the biggest fish in the ocean.'

'Well, good luck to her,' Emma said darkly. 'I hope that she has the patience of Job. She'll need it if she's going to put up with Conrad DeVere for more than five minutes.'

They drove back in a silence broken only by the odd remark from Sophia, who seemed only mildly disconcerted by Conrad's terseness. She lay back with her head against the cushioned headrest, her eyes closed behind the large sunglasses, her face upraised to the sun which filtered through the glass into the air-conditioned car.

When they arrived back at the house, Lloyd drew her to one side, reiterating his offer to show her around Trinidad if she ever decided to pay it a visit. He was travelling back early the following morning.

'Can't stay away from my nightclub for too long,' he whispered conspiratorially in her ear. 'All those girls. I can't deprive them of my masterful company or else they start pining.'

'You live in a dream world, Lloyd,' Emma whispered back.

'I know, but it's fun, isn't it?'

Out of the corner of her eye Emma could see Conrad watching their brief parting exchange with a grim expression.

He nodded to them as they drove off, and Emma followed him into the house. In the sort of mood that he was in, avoidance was obviously the best policy. It had been an enjoyable afternoon, only marred by Conrad's ill temper. If he were less formidable a man, it could quite easily have been ignored, but his personality dominated everything and he had made no effort to hide his curtness.

Emma ran quickly up the staircase. Conrad was nowhere to be seen, which was just as well because he was about the last person she wanted to confront.

She mentally planned the rest of what remained of her day, deciding that she would sit with Alistair for as long as he wanted. They still had a lot to discuss, reminiscences which she would enjoy hearing about, if he did not find them too painful. There was much he could tell her and as much that she could tell him.

Her bedroom door was ajar when she reached her room. Emma wondered fleetingly whether Esther had been in to clean the room and forgotten to close it.

She pushed it open, her mind still racing ahead to all the things that Alistair and she had to say to each other.

Conrad was lying on the bed, in a pair of shorts and the same T-shirt which he had worn to the beach and which clung to his body in damp patches. His hands were clasped behind his head and he was surveying her through narrowed eyes.

Emma stopped in her tracks, feeling the adrenalin pumping quickly through her body. Her mouth went dry and the fine blonde hairs on her arms almost seemed to stand on end.

'What are you doing here?' she asked warily. 'What do you want?' She stopped where she was, not daring to take another step forwards. It would bring her too close to him.

She had already seen what he was capable of—worse, what she was capable of with him—and the prospect of a repeat performance of what had happened that morning frightened her.

The hooded blue eyes gazing at her sent little alarm bells ringing in her head, even though she told herself that she could control the situation.

But she didn't like the way he was looking at her. It was far too intense and far too stripping.

He's got a fiancée, she thought wildly, trying to compose her features into ordered calm.

She thought of Sophia, but the image was blurry.

'Would you mind leaving?' she said coolly. 'I want to change.'

'Feel free.' Conrad gestured expansively towards the ensuite bathroom, but did not budge.

'I'd feel freer if you left.'

They stared at each other for what seemed to Emma like decades. She could feel the heavy pounding of her heart, could almost hear it, and she wondered whether he could hear it too.

'You mean if someone else were here instead?'

Emma regarded him in frank puzzlement. 'Someone else?' she repeated. 'What are you talking about?'

'You know very well what I'm talking about,' Conrad replied roughly. He slung his legs over the side of the bed and was standing in front of her before Emma could even realise what was happening.

She looked around desperately at the half-opened door. He followed the line of her gaze and closed it gently but firmly.

'You intrigue me. So cool and composed. I might have guessed that I was wrong. You proved that to me this morning. There's a fire burning in you. Were you hoping Lloyd would ignite it the way I did? You were all over each other. I'm surprised you managed to restrain yourself in the back seat of the car. Is he your sort of man?'

'More than you are, at any rate,' Emma bit out recklessly.

'How would you know? One kiss wasn't enough.'

Before she knew what was happening he bent his head towards her, his hand curling into her hair, drawing her face up to meet his.

With a muffled moan, Emma twisted her body to try and get away, but he gripped her closer to him, his lips devouring hers hungrily.

Emma felt herself sway. Her legs seemed to have suddenly turned to water. In fact, every nerve in her body seemed suddenly to have turned to water.

As his mouth moved over hers, the feverish greed of his kiss becoming more persuasive, she felt any semblance of self-control that she might have had slipping away from her, like grains of sand through an open hand. She closed her eyes and closed her mind from her normal processes of reasoning.

With a soft moan, half proclaiming her resistance, she succumbed to the searing intensity of his kiss, returning it with equal fervour.

Be reasonable, she thought wildly, but she couldn't because it felt as though this was what she had been waiting for. He had given her a taste of passion and she was thirsty for more. No man had ever sent these tremors through her body. Her tongue met his and she felt as if she was drowning in something over which she had no control.

Her hands met behind his neck, her fingers weaving into his black hair. As his mouth bit against her neck she arched back, groaning softly as the spasms of pleasure tore through her.

She felt his hand move up her back, searing like red-hot embers through the thin material of her jersey. She was terrified by her loss of self-control. Was she so weak that she could abandon herself with such mindless oblivion to a man who was engaged? Someone whose opinion of her did not bear thinking about?

She should have been prepared for this. Her body, which she had always trusted to obey her commands, had forsaken her this morning, and the experience should have warned her. It should have shown her that his power to make her respond against her will was formidable.

She made an effort to pull away, but as their bodies disengaged slightly he slipped his hand over her breast, caressing it through the still damp swimsuit. With an impatient tug, he eased down the top, moaning as his hand came into contact with her naked skin. Her breasts hardened at his touch, her nipples taut as he rubbed them between his fingers.

Her eyes opened and she stared dazedly at him. He looked at her, and must have read the yearning on her face, because he eased her jersey off, his mouth trailing from her neck to her breasts.

His breathing was ragged, as ragged as her own was. She pushed him away from her, her mind finally engaging into gear. She thought of Sophia, and remembered where his allegiances lay. She must have been crazy to even let him touch her, far less to have responded with the hot excitement that she had.

'Let me go!' she muttered, pulling up her swimsuit so that it covered her breasts.

Conrad looked at her uncomprehendingly.

'Have you forgotten that you're engaged?' she asked, her voice rising in self-disgust and anger. 'Get out of my room!' She wished that the ground would just open and swallow her up. In a minute she would burst into tears, and that was the very last thing she wanted him to witness.

'God, Emma, I don't want to.' His hand stroked her thigh. From under her lashes, Emma gazed at the warm curve of his mouth. Her legs were dissolving. If she didn't do something soon, all thought of the rights and wrongs of what she was doing would vanish like a puff of smoke. 'I want this ice maiden to dissolve in my lovemaking.'

'You're engaged,' she said in a high, desperate voice.

'Engagements are made to be broken,' he whispered ambiguously.

Emma didn't have a clue what he was talking about. His words filtered into her brain and promptly evaporated under the heated response of her body to his.

She held his wrist tightly, until she could feel her nails biting into his skin.

'This isn't for me,' she said shakily. 'Please leave.'

'Don't make me.'

'If you don't let go of me now, right now, I'm going to scream until you do.'

It took everything in her to say it, and she didn't feel any better. His hand was warm and trembling slightly, and the only thing she wanted to do was to feel it move over every inch of her body.

The drowsy passion in Conrad's eyes was slowly being replaced by incomprehension, as though she had thrown a bucket of ice-cold water over his head.

'Are you telling me that you don't want me?' he muttered.

'I'm telling you to leave this room before I scream the house down! Is this your ploy for getting me out of here? If it is, then it's working, because there's no way that I'm going to stay here if I have to be on the look-out for you all of the time!'

She thought of Sophia, and was relieved when she felt the anger building up inside of her. Anger was a safe emotion as far as Conrad was concerned. She could cope with that.

'Stop playing the innocent,' he bit out in a voice as furious as hers. 'I didn't exactly see you dashing for help.'

She had recovered completely now, and was rapidly gathering together the strands of her composure which had been scattered to the winds.

'And you dare call Lloyd a womaniser.' She spoke in a cold, calm voice. 'Well, you're a womaniser of the worst sort. Now get out of this room.'

He stared at her, speechless, and then turned on his heel. As the door closed behind him, Emma felt her body sag as though she had been held by strings which had suddenly been cut. She sank on to the bed and wondered what was happening to her.

She knew of course. Her subconscious had known for a long time. She was attracted to him. Why deny it? She had been attracted to him perhaps from the very first moment she clapped eyes on him. Seeing him with Sophia, knowing that he had most probably made love to her, had been agonising.

One of a queue, she thought cynically. She had hoped that his engagement would put things into perspective, show her what kind of fool she was being, but it hadn't. Admit it, she said to herself: you're a weak fool.

She relived the sensation of his body pressed against hers and his hands stroking her body with a shudder of disgust.

Sexual attraction, infatuation; call it what you want, she thought, it was an illness, a disease which she could overcome.

Or, if not overcome, then at least control. The man was a bastard, a dangerous, sexually mesmerising bastard. She had *thought* him a threat before. Now she knew that he was one.

CHAPTER SIX

EMMA'S body was still trembling when she stepped into the shower five minutes later. She numbly felt the hard jet of water streaming over her, cleaning everthing except what mattered, the part inside her which needed, as far as she was concerned, more than cleansing. It needed disinfecting.

Face it, she concluded miserably: the man was right when he said that she had let him do everything that he had. Worse, she had enjoyed it. She had relished the feel of him, all the sensations that had rippled through her as his hands and fingers had explored her body.

How long had she been waiting to touch him? She dressed slowly, deliberately choosing clothes in dull, muted colours, because that was how she felt inside.

It took a huge effort to pretend to Alistair, when she went to visit him, that there was nothing wrong.

'Are you sure?' he insisted, frowning. 'You look peaky.'

'I must have taken too much sun this afternoon,' Emma hedged vaguely, launching into an extended account of how she had spent the day, omitting all mention of Conrad. She knew from experience how Alistair responded to his name, and the last thing she needed was to spend an hour and a half talking about him. He had eaten away enough of her already.

By the end of the evening she felt totally drained and ready for bed. She had no idea where Conrad was, had asked no one, and was only grateful for his absence.

Coward, she told herself; you're going to have to face him some time, although every second that he was not around was a second more for her to reconstruct her barricade, her invisible protection.

Now that she knew what she was up against, maybe she could manage a little more successfully to slap down any wayward attraction, because there was no way that she had any intention of giving in furthur to her own frightening craving for him.

Had she learnt nothing at all from her mother? After her disastrous and brief marriage to her father, she had spent the rest of her life seemingly drawn to all those men from whom she should have been running as fast as she could. Towards the end, she had given up completely and resigned herself to the fact that stability and enduring love would always be beyond her grasp. It had only been her sense of humour that had saved her from becoming an embittered woman.

Emma had seen it and had learnt from it. Or, at least, she'd thought she had. Certainly if she had had any sense she would have left the island the minute she clapped eyes on Conrad DeVere. She had had too much faith in her own inner strength, and too little in his overwhelming and magnetic sex appeal.

It helped when Esther informed her in passing that she would be on her own that evening, as Conrad had gone to see Sophia and her parents.

It came as no surprise. Through the open kitchen window she had noticed that his car was missing, and it didn't take a fool to put two and two together. He had hardly decided to go for a drive to the beach so that he could look at the moonlight.

Oh, no. Not him. Not Conrad DeVere. Why look at the moonlight when he could take the quickest route to Sophia's house and finish what he had begun with Emma?

Something inside her whispered that he was not that type of man, but she paid no attention to it. It made things infinitely easier if she believed the very worst of him, and she needed all the help she could get.

For the first time since she had arrived on the island she slept badly, waking up several times to a feeling of disorientation in the inky blackness of the bedroom.

The face that stared back at her the following morning in the mirror was a true reflection of her state of mind. There were shadows underneath her eyes; even the tan seemed to have deserted her.

With grim determination, she carefully applied a layer of make-up, much more than she normally used, until she at least resembled something human. Her hair she drew back into a thick ponytail with a piece of black elastic.

She knew exactly how she would occupy herself for the morning. No beach, no relaxation, nothing so lazy and enjoyable. She did not want to enjoy herself at all. In some obscure way she thought that it would help if she punished herself, so after a light breakfast she quickly visited Alistair—who, although considerably brighter than he had been, now seemed to have developed the habit of pitifully referring to his advanced years—and then vanished into the study.

There was not much to do. She had finished all the typing which had been on her agenda a few days, so she painstakingly revised her work and then set about rooting through the books, devouring as much literature on Alistair's life as she could. There was a surprising amount of cuttings, some dating back further than she had expected. Emma read it all, slowly and carefully, making the time spin out as much as she could.

It was interesting reading about the man whom she was beginning to know so well, trying to fit together the pieces of his personality as seen in black and white against the flesh-and-blood old man lying in his bed upstairs. Wasn't there a wide variance? she mused. Only the factual side of his life could be relied upon as being the truth.

She was so engrossed in her detective work that when the phone clanged next to her Emma physically jumped and looked at it in surprise.

It was Sophia on the other end. She sounded breathless and slightly hesitant as she asked whether Conrad was back yet.

'I have no idea,' Emma replied truthfully.

There was a pause on the other end, 'Can you tell him that I called?'

Emma promised, glancing at her watch which showed that it had gone twelve o'clock. 'I could go and see whether I can find him for you,' she said reluctantly, relieved when the other girl told her not to bother.

'It's just that I'm flying out to Rome this afternoon,' Sophia explained.

'And you wanted to talk to him before you left.' Why wait for her to say it? Emma thought. If she volunteered the information herself, then it somehow made her feel more in control.

'Yes,' Sophia agreed, 'I wanted to tell him that I was sorry about how things ended.'

'I'll tell him.' Emma felt a thread of curiosity streak through her, but she was determined not to give in to it. She had already given in to too much as far as Conrad was concerned. Her first step in fighting off that desperate attraction towards him which threatened to engulf her, was to have as little to do with him, and as little to say about him, as possible.

'Don't you want to know what I'm talking about?' Sophia asked.

'Not really.'

'Well——' Sophia began, and Emma thought, Oh, no, here we go. She could recognise the lowered voice of someone who wanted to confess, to pour their heart out.

Emma had been the confidante of her friends too many times for her not to see the signs.

This time, she did not want to be on the receiving end. There was too much locked up inside her which she would have liked to burden someone with, but couldn't. It wasn't simply that her friends were all thousands of miles away. The fact was that she had made too much of a habit of her aloofness, had cultivated her privacy for too long, for her to suddenly break it.

'You needn't talk to me about this,' she said with a hint of desperation in her voice.

'I know, but it's just that I haven't anyone else to tell. Besides, sometimes it's easier talking to a stranger than to a friend.' Sophia fell silent, as though she was trying to put her thoughts into some kind of sequence. 'It's just that I broke off the engagement and I wanted to make sure that we were still friends. I feel so badly about it, but I chatted to Lloyd about it when he was here, and I decided that I just wasn't ready for marriage. Besides, an important job came up.'

'An important job?' Wasn't marriage an important job? Emma wondered.

Sophia's tone relaxed, began to sound more confident and enthusiastic. 'A chance-in-a-lifetime opportunity, really. I got offered a contract to work for a cosmetic firm, and part of the agreement was no attachment to the opposite sex for a year. So you see, there was nothing really that I could do.'

'Of course,' Emma said with mild sarcasm. 'When exactly did you tell Conrad?'

'At the beach yesterday. Well, I sort of told him then. We talked about it properly yesterday evening—but it was while you and Lloyd were swimming that I sort of hinted . . .'

'Ah, I see.' And she did. No wonder he was in such a filthy mood on the drive back. It made sense.

'Of course,' Sophia said confidentially, and Emma could imagine her adopting a suitable pose by the telephone, 'I'll be missing out on all the security I would have had married to a man like Conrad. I mean, he's *the* catch around. Handsome, powerful, and of course rich, rich, rich. Not just his money, but he'll probably get all of Alistair's money as well. Still——' she sighed theatrically '—that's life, as my dearest brother would say.'

She chatted inconsequentially about Lloyd, but Emma didn't hear what she was saying. She felt faint. Alistair's money? Did he think he was going to inherit Alistair's money? He had never suggested anything of the kind, but if Sophia was as nonchalant about disclosing such information, then surely it must be based on fact. No smoke without fire.

Tiny, suspicious thoughts were buzzing in her head, irritating insects which refused to go away. Emma blinked and shook her head to clear it.

'Anyway, could you pass on the message?' Almost before Emma had had a chance to agree, the other girl had rung off, and Emma held the receiver away from her ear, absent-mindedly hearing the flat, purring dialling tone.

She replaced the receiver thoughtfully, no longer in any mood to pore over old journals and newspaper clippings.

The nagging uncertainties were becoming too persistent, the buzzing of one bee developing into a swarm. She didn't want to listen to them. After all, they were hardly based on fact, and Sophia might have been completely wrong in her assumptions—but then again, they answered a lot of questions.

For instance, was that the real reason for Conrad's initial reaction to her? Had he seen her as more than simply a potential threat to Alistair? Had he seen her as a potential threat to him as well?

She went out to the garden and looked admiringly at the flowers and plants, her mind somewhere else.

Anyway, she thought, it didn't matter one way or the other, because she really didn't care what the man thought of her.

She tried to relax and enjoy the warm, salty sea breeze rustling through the coconut trees and the hibiscus plants, but it was with a depressing feeling of inevitability that she saw Conrad's car pull up the long driveway. She had no intention of initiating a conversation with him. She watched him lever his long body out of the driver's seat and gave him a false, syrupy smile as he approached her.

He didn't smile back.

'Super garden,' Emma said conversationally, refusing to be rattled either by the hard set of his face or her disconcerting train of thoughts. It annoyed her that, however suspicious she was of him, she still could not prevent her physical awareness of him. 'Can you believe this variety of flowers? It's almost like being at the Chelsea Flower Show. I made an effort once to cultivate the small patch at the back of the house at home, but I soon discovered that I didn't have green fingers. Only when it came to the weeds, at any rate.' The small talk was dying on her lips, and she flashed him another brilliant smile.

She could feel the pulse in her neck throbbing with painful intensity and she kept her eyes riveted to his face. There was no way that she would let herself drink in the lean muscularity of his body. That would conjure up too many graphic images of it pressed against hers, his thighs hard and demanding, his hands feverishly raking her back and breasts.

'I've just seen the doctor,' he said bluntly. 'I passed him on the way back and stopped for a chat.'

Emma's eyes widened in surprise. She had had no idea that Doctor Tompkins had been to the house, but then she had been so absorbed in her work that she had not been aware of very much outside it.

'What did he say?' she asked quickly. 'I didn't even know that he had been. I was working all morning.'

'No change, and he still refuses to elaborate on the seriousness of Alistair's condition. I can't drag a thing out of him. He just keeps wittering on about the rights of the patient, and that it was Alistair's decision to tell us or not to tell us exactly what's going on.'

They had begun walking back to the house, Emma keeping a reasonable distance away from him.

She had wondered whether he would mention their lovemaking the day before, but apparently not. She thought bitterly that it meant so little to him that it was not even worth a passing word. He would put the whole thing down to experience, if he hadn't forgotten about it all already.

She had probably been no more than a trivial diversion for him. He would have willingly and expertly made love to her to take his mind off his rejection by Sophia and, when she had come to her senses and made him leave, would have put the whole episode out of his mind like an irksome dream.

How was he to know that every touch from him was now embedded in her heart, like some virulent stranglehold?

The women he dated, the women he made love to, she forced herself to think, were women of experience. He and they satiated themselves with each other and then moved on, like trains flashing past each other in the dead of night.

The fact that she could not forget just showed what a gullible fool she was.

Well, two could play at that game. She could be as cool as he was, even if it took everything out of her. There was no way that she would let him see how much he had affected her. She would cling on to the remnants of her pride if it was the last thing she did.

So she listened to him with a forced, tinny smile.

'What can we do?' she asked. 'If Alistair refuses to divulge exactly how serious his condition is, then we have no choice but to accept it.'

'You accept a lot, don't you?' he asked with a strange inflexion in his voice. 'All with that cool little face of yours.'

Emma felt her heart beating heavily against her ribcage and she said airily, 'I try.'

The atmosphere thickened between them and, to break it, Emma commented in a neutral voice that Sophia had called. 'To apologise about the engagement,' she added tonelessly.

'So she told you, did she?'

'She told me that she'd broken it off, yes.' And more. I hope, she thought silently, that it's wrecked your ego. She glanced across at him, but he did not look like a man whose ego had taken a beating.

He shrugged. 'It was mutual.'

'Was that why you were so abrupt and ill-humoured at the beach yesterday?' Emma could not resist asking coldly.

'At the beach?' He looked at her sharply. 'What are you talking about?'

You know what I'm talking about, she wanted to scream. Instead she said calmly, 'Sophia said that she began to tell you that she couldn't go through with the marriage yesterday at the beach.'

'Oh, yes, so she did,' he agreed.

'Faced with the choice of an offer from a cosmetics firm and an offer from you, she plumped for the better one,' Emma pressed. If she wanted to drive the point home and stir a reaction from him, she failed. He nodded agreeably but didn't seem in the least perturbed by the implication.

'She has her career to think of,' he said, pushing the front door open so that Emma could walk through. She brushed past him, feeling her pulses quicken at his proximity.

Didn't anything put a dent in this man's staggering self-confidence? And he talked about her coolness! Of course, he had mentioned that calling off the engagement had been mutual, but he had not elaborated. Maybe it was his own way of saving face, but he was not behaving like a man trying to justify a broken relationship.

'I think we should both go and see Alistair and try and figure out exactly what's going on,' Conrad said, relegating the whole subject of himself and Sophia to the past.

Emma nodded. She would have liked to have continued the discussion—she would have taken an almost masochistic pleasure in it—but she already knew him well enough to realise that he would divulge no more than he wanted to.

Alistair was in his wheelchair when they entered the bedroom, a book in one hand, a cup of coffee in the other. He had obviously not expected them and glanced sheepishly at the bed.

'You're looking better,' Conrad said drily, sitting on the old flowered sofa in the corner of the room. He patted the free seat next to him and Emma reluctantly sat down, primly crossing her legs at the ankles.

'I'm still a sick man,' Alistair mumbled, sipping out of his coffee-cup.

He glanced coyly at both of them, and said in a weak voice, 'I'm better for having my lovely granddaughter here, of course, but I'm still ill. The doctor tells me so, anyway.'

'Which brings us to the point in question,' Conrad said smoothly. 'The doctor. He refuses to say anything, leaving it up to you. Except that you haven't exactly been a fount of information either. So what's the story? How ill are you?'

'I've already told you,' Alistair complained evasively. He threw Emma a watery smile and asked her if she'd like Esther to bring up another tray with coffee and biscuits.

Conrad shook his head. 'You're avoiding the subject again, Alistair.'

'Perish the thought.'

'So, in words of one syllable, tell me what the doctor said. Is it your heart playing up again?'

Emma knew that Alistair had a heart condition. He had spoken to her about it, but he had not mentioned that that was at the bottom of his current problem. In retrospect, she realised that he had swept aside all mention of his illness with suave caginess.

'Something like that,' Alistair mumbled testily. 'I won't bore you with the details.'

'Please,' Conrad persisted, 'bore us.' He looked at Emma and glanced upwards. Without realising it, she dropped her mask and grinned.

'Well,' Alistair began, 'it's the old ticker. Not as strong as it used to be. The doctor said that I shouldn't get any shocks. A pleasant surprise might be nice, though—might revive me. I mean,' he added hastily, 'Emma's revelation was wonderful, a rush of spring air into an old man's bones, but as you can see I'm still very much under the weather. So the doctor tells me.'

'Very informative, Doctor Tompkins,' Conrad said wryly. 'His advice sounds very much like the sort of advice you'd prescribe for yourself.'

Alistair made an indeterminate sound.

'Well, no doubt you'll find this a pleasant surprise. Sophia and I are no longer an issue.'

Alistair's eyes gleamed under the bushy brows. 'All off, is it? Just as well, my boy. The two of you weren't suited at all, as I've told you often enough before. I'm just glad that you came to your senses in time. You know what they say: marry in haste, repent at leisure.'

He was smiling broadly.

'Still, you were right on one count, it's high time you settled down.'

'We've covered this ground already, Alistair. Don't tell me that you're growing repetitive in your old age.'

'It breaks an old man's heart to think that he might die without seeing you settled. Your father would have wanted it.'

Conrad frowned, a shadow of doubt crossing his face.

'We mustn't keep you. You're beginning to look tired.' Emma rose and walked towards the door.

When Conrad joined her a few minutes later, he looked unusually unsure.

'I just don't know what to make of him,' he said thoughtfully. 'If I didn't know better, I'd have said that there was nothing wrong with the old warrior, but there's no doubt that he did have a turn when we were at that damned party, and who's to tell how serious it was? The wily old devil's certainly not letting on.'

'But why shouldn't he?'

'Why indeed?'

Emma thought she knew why. He simply didn't want to worry either of them. He especially didn't want to upset her, knowing as he did that she was still suffering from the death of her mother, but there was no way that she was going to put forward this theory, not with that cynical glint in Conrad's eyes. He naturally wouldn't give her the benefit of the doubt, and the very last thing she wanted was an argument with him. In fact, the very last thing she wanted was to be with him at all, especially now.

When they reached the sitting-room, she branched out with the excuse that there was still some unfinished work left for her to do.

'Really?' Conrad said disbelievingly. 'You must be a much slower worker than I thought.'

He turned his back to walk away and as he did so Emma glimpsed a faint smile on his lips.

He never gave up, did he? she thought, simmering with anger. He obviously found his own sense of humour at her expense highly entertaining. She slammed into the study and through sheer perversity spent the next two hours doing what could quite easily have been done in twenty minutes.

She was relaxing back in the leather swivel chair, her eyes closed, when the door opened and Conrad walked into the study. He lightly swivelled her chair round, and Emma's eyes flew open.

'Thanks for knocking,' she muttered.

'I did.' Conrad's blue eyes mocked her.

'Well, it must have been very softly,' Emma snapped. 'I didn't hear a thing. What do you want, anyway?'

Conrad looked at her with mock hurt, but she could see from the twist of his lips that he still found it highly amusing to have burst in on her and found her half asleep in the chair.

It crossed her mind that he must really wonder what she was doing to justify her pay packet, and she immediately decided that, since he wasn't employing her, then it didn't matter.

'That's not very polite. Especially when I came to ask you out to dinner.'

'Dinner?' Emma eyed him in frank amazement.

'That's right. I know a very good restaurant not too far from here—close to the airport, believe it or not.'

'I can't make it,' Emma replied spontaneously. Dinner with Conrad spelt trouble.

'Why not? Don't tell me you've got other plans for the evening.'

'Esther will already have prepared something,' she fudged. 'It's after six o'clock.'

Conrad smiled, but his eyes were intent on her. 'I told her not to. She's going to do something light for Alistair.'

'How nice of you to arrange the evening for me on my behalf,' Emma commented coldly. She felt like a rabbit caught in a trap. The glint in Conrad's eyes told her plainly enough that he was not going to take no for an answer—not that she could come up with any kind of excuse, anyway.

'There's something I want to talk to you about,' he said flatly, 'so you can stop trying to wriggle out of it. I've booked a table for eight, so we'll have to leave by seven-thirty. I'll meet you downstairs, and be prompt. I have an aversion to being kept waiting.'

With that parting shot he let himself out of the room, and Emma regarded the closed door with a sinking feeling. She had no idea what he wanted to talk about but she resented his presumption that it overrode any plans that she might have made, even if her plans were only to wash her hair and retire early to bed with a good book.

She lingered over her bath, topping up the water three times until she felt that if she didn't get out she would emerge looking like a dried-out prune.

She was already beginning to feel slightly apprehensive about being so close to Conrad without any easy escape routes to hand. She didn't trust herself. Not after the last time.

With a sigh of resignation she picked out what she was going to wear. A full rose-coloured skirt with a snug-fitting matching bodice buttoned down the front, which revealed as little of her as possible. With a flash of inspiration, she tied her hair back with a bright scarf which she had picked up on one of her rare jaunts into Scarborough, the capital of the island, and made up with a little blusher and eyeshadow.

When she stood back from the mirror, she was pleased with the overall effect.

Conrad was waiting at the foot of the stairs for her. She saw him before he had a chance to look around, and in that brief moment she allowed herself the luxury of watching him unobserved.

He really was blatantly masculine. His face was turned away from her, his hands thrust into the pockets of his charcoal-grey trousers, but even in that attitude he was arresting.

He looked around as she began descending the stairs, carefully because she was wearing higher shoes than normal. From this distance, she couldn't make out the expression on his face but she was aware that he was staring at her, and this time there was no smile on his lips.

She wondered what was going through that head of his. He must have seen a million women descending flights of staircases to meet him, in hotels, in mansions, at clubs, but even so the way that he was looking at her made her nervously self-conscious.

He looked at her as though she filled his senses, but of course she wasn't completely dim. Wasn't that part and parcel of the inveterate charmer? To treat a woman with undivided attention, as though she was the only one in the world? She stared back into his brooding, black-fringed eyes politely.

'I'm not late,' she offered brightly.

Conrad's serious expression didn't alter. 'So I see,' he drawled, 'though it would have been well worth the wait.'

'Thank you,' Emma stammered. Out of sheer embarrassment she began chatting quickly, asking him questions about the restaurant, about Tobago in general. Anything to have the conversation flowing on a level which she found manageable.

Once in the car she relaxed in the darkness, and let her thoughts drift over Alistair, his illness, Conrad, and her own feelings towards them. Where would it all end? It was amazing to think that less than six months ago she had been in London, far away from all this. And before that... before that there had not even been any thoughts of Alistair at all, except as a shadowy figure whom her mother intermittently mentioned. Emma had no more expected to meet him than she had expected to meet Superman, even though she had speculated about him and the rift that had formed between her mother and him.

At least, from the point of view of Alistair, the journey had been worth it.

If in the process she had managed to ignite feelings which she had not even known existed, then it was something she would have to live with.

Besides, physical attraction didn't last. It was heady while it was there, but the effects wore off sooner or later, like the effects from drinking too much good wine. Conrad had succeeded in knocking her for six, but she would recover. It was no more than a sexual attraction, powerful though it might be.

The restaurant turned out to double as a small hotel as well, with guest quarters scattered among the creeping bougainvillaea and set back from the swimming pool.

They were shown to their table in what Emma conceded had to be the most charming setting imaginable. The restaurant was simply a small cluster of tables and chairs set in two circular, open spaces which were sheltered from the rain by thatched roofs supported on wooden beams.

The proprietor came over to them, delighting Emma when he told her that in the mornings the guests would breakfast to the accompaniment of the tropical birds which flew to the tables on the offchance of nipping some fallen crumbs of bread.

'It's idyllic,' Emma breathed to Conrad, when they were looking at their menus. 'So much nicer than those dreadful dark rooms in England that try and rake up a phony intimate atmosphere.' She wanted to add that intimacy was where they were now, sitting at tables from which she could see the stars and the moon, but she refrained.

'Glad you accepted my offer, then?' In the flickering light of the candle, she saw him smile drily at her, and her nerves raced.

'Did I have much choice?' she rejoined lightly. 'This place really is exquisite, though. And yes, I'm glad I came.'

She read the menu with interest, settling for the local dish of the day, and relaxed in her seat. The silence between them was comfortable and she had a brief, aching sensation of never having been so happy before.

Over the meal, Conrad talked to her about his business, about his interests and about a hundred other little things in a way that was amusing and informative.

As the proprietor brought them their coffee, he leaned back against the chair and looked at her leisurely through narrowed eyes.

'Aren't you going to get around to asking what it was I wanted to talk to you about?'

Emma looked at him, suddenly realising that she had completely forgotten the point of the evening. She had been so taken with the wine, the easy flow of conversation, the unreal atmosphere, that his question brought her sharply back down to earth.

'I was about to get around to it,' she lied, twirling the stem of her glass. For some reason she felt wary. Whatever he was about to say was serious. It was written on the sculptured contours of his face.

'It's about Alistair, actually,' he began, and Emma frowned, puzzled. Was that why he had brought her here? To talk about Alistair? She thought that they had covered all that already, and, even if they hadn't, surely it could have been discussed back at the villa?

'You mean his illness?' she asked, baffled.

Conrad nodded. 'Basically, yes,' he concurred. 'It doesn't appear that he's getting any better. True enough, he's not getting any worse, and it's undoubtedly helped knowing that you're his granddaughter, and having you around, but I would have thought that he'd be making more of an effort to get back into the swing of things by now. He's never been one to let his ill health get the better of him. He's a great believer in the power of the fighting spirit. How else would he ever have risen to where he was if he hadn't believed in his own strength of mind?' He paused as though rehearsing in his head what he was about to say.

'Maybe you'll believe me when I say that he's iller than he's letting on,' Emma interrupted. 'Isn't it like him to try and make light of something serious?'

'I've given it some thought,' Conrad agreed, 'and I think that maybe you're right.'

Now that he had said it, Emma felt a chill sweep through her. It made the seriousness of Alistair's condition all the more painful. She realised with a start that Conrad's confidence that he was going to be all right had influenced her reaction more than she had admitted. She had had an inexplicable faith in what he said, like a child who instinctively believed an adult.

Silly, of course, especially as he was now agreeing with what she had suspected all along.

'If the prospect of continuing with his work isn't enough to get him out of that bed,' Conrad stated bluntly, 'then there's only one thing that will.'

'There is?' Emma repeated sceptically. If there was, then she sure as hell couldn't think of it.

Conrad stared at her impatiently, like a detective waiting for his loyal assistant to arrive at the right conclusion. When she continued to look at him blankly, he said flatly, 'Yes. You know what he wants so badly. Have all his none too subtle innuendoes gone completely over your head?'

Emma shook her head slowly. A nebulous thought was beginning to take shape, but it couldn't be...

'I can tell you see what I'm driving at. We're going to have to convince him that we're engaged and about to be married.'

CHAPTER SEVEN

'YOU'RE joking, aren't you.' It wasn't a question, it was a statement. Emma looked at Conrad, waiting for him to agree, to nod, to laugh, to do *anything* except sit there, unsmiling.

'I've never been more serious in my life.' He meant it, too, she could see that.

'But you can't be! It's the most ridiculous idea I've ever heard. It's ludicrous, absurd, downright stupid!' The words were tripping over each other. Emma gulped a mouthful of tepid coffee and made a face. On the few occasions that she had contemplated marriage, she had never once thought that it would be this way. Of course, men these days were practical; they proposed casually—going down on bended knee had been relegated to a thing of the past—but this was going too far.

She looked at him stubbornly, refusing to believe that he wasn't suddenly going to burst out laughing.

'Why is it ridiculous?' Conrad asked, his clever face scrutinising hers, almost as though *she* was the one who needed humouring.

'Why? I could think of a thousand reasons why!'

'Fine. Tell me about them.' He stretched back and looked at her patiently.

'All right,' she replied hotly, 'how's this for starters? He'll never in a month of Sundays believe us. I mean, it's hardly as though we hit it off from the start, is it? Don't you think he might just ask himself how come we've suddenly decided that we want to get married? One minute we're arguing with each other, the next minute we've decided that we'll celebrate our differences by getting engaged! Don't you think it's a bit extreme? Would you buy that if you were in his position? However much you wanted to believe it?'

It sounded convincing enough, and she sat back triumphantly. Her heart was beating fast, so fast that if she hadn't known better she would have thought that the mere idea of being married to Conrad, of pretending, for heaven's sake, was enough to excite her.

Of course, that in itself was ludicrous.

'Why wouldn't he believe us?' Conrad asked lazily. 'Don't you think we can convince him that we're madly in love? I do.'

Emma flushed. 'You must be a good actor, then.' When he didn't reply, she rushed on, 'Anyway, even if by some miracle of short-sightedness he *did* believe us, what then?'

'I don't follow you.'

'What makes you think that it'll make a scrap of difference to his health?'

She didn't know why she was even bothering to pursue this line of conversation, but now that she had started she realised with alarm that it was becoming increasingly difficult to back down. She should have laughed the whole thing off from the start and simply refused to consider it.

'Think about it,' Conrad said in a patient voice that made her want to scream. 'He's been going on about it in one way or another for ages. If he thinks that his dream is finally going to be realised, it would give him something to live for, something to start recuperating for.'

Put like that, it made sense in a weird sort of way. The sensation of sinking was getting stronger. Emma rooted around for more objections. People didn't *pretend* to be getting married, for God's sake. She didn't know anyone who had ever *pretended* to be getting married.

Trust him, she thought, to come up with a fool scheme like that. His sharp mind was just the kind to bypass normal convention and settle on the quickest route possible, regardless of everyday scruples.

'I don't have to think about it. I can tell you without giving it any thought at all that I don't like the idea. He's my grandfather, and I just don't like the thought of deceiving him. It's underhand and it's dishonest.'

'You'd prefer to see him ill?'

Emma glared at him. Not only was he a dab hand at manipulating people, she thought sourly, he was pretty adept at manipulating words as well. He made her sound as though she was uncaring, merely because she had a few scruples!

'Of course I don't want to see him ill!' she retorted. 'I suffered enough when my mother died. Do you really think I don't feel scared stiff that I might suffer again if Alistair's condition worsens? It's just that what you're suggesting is unscrupulous.' In fact, typical.

'You don't think that the end justifies the means? If Alistair needs this push to recover, then I'm willing to do it.'

'Well,' Emma said sweetly, staring at Conrad's dark, brooding face, 'isn't that big of you? Of course, you're well used to arranged marriages, but have you thought that I might not be?'

'I would have thought,' he murmured equally smoothly, 'that you would have agreed to anything that might help him. You're his granddaughter, dammit. Naturally, I could be mistaken. Your great show of concern and affection might not be as genuine as you would have us all believe. It might just be a convincing little act, so that you can contrive to get some of Alistair's wealth to rub off on you.' His voice was soft, but he was watching her intently, his mouth set in a grim line.

Emma knew precisely what was going on in that head of his and she didn't like it. He had opted for the one argument that was guaranteed to squash any further disagreements from her, and had pulled it out like a card which he had been keeping up his sleeve.

'That's not fair,' she mumbled, staring defeat in the face.

He smiled, a slow, relaxed smile, like a tiger that had successfully cornered its prey. He signalled for the bill, not taking his eyes off her face.

'All right, and what if he recovers?'

'When.'

'Have it your way. What do we do *when* he recovers?'

'We can cross that bridge when we get to it. Is that it for your objections?'

Emma didn't answer.

'So that's settled, then?' he asked as they prepared to leave the restaurant.

Emma disgruntledly wondered why he even bothered to ask the question. He knew that her answer was no longer in the balance. 'So it seems,' she replied coolly.

'Good.'

They drove back in silence, Emma too preoccupied with her thoughts to have even the slightest interest in the dense, lush undergrowth darkly shifting around them.

When the car pulled up outside the house, Conrad switched off the engine and looked at her, his arm resting along the seat behind her head. Emma instinctively edged away.

'We'll see him tomorrow, first thing.'

Emma mumbled her agreement.

'And make it convincing.'

She forbore to comment, instead clanking open the car door and walking quickly towards the house. She waited while Conrad leisurely locked up the car and then sauntered to join her, taking much longer than necessary to open the front door.

He's enjoying this, she thought. He's enjoying knowing that he's thrown me into an untenable position. The fact that she was angry was giving him the greatest of pleasure.

As soon as the door was open, she ran up the stairs towards her bedroom, ignoring Conrad's voice as he called out to her, 'No thanks for an enjoyable evening, then?'

The man was a sadist, she decided, once she was alone in the privacy of her bedroom. Fortune had definitely been having a laugh at her expense when the damned man had decided to take a break for some rest and relaxation. Why couldn't he have had a shorter break, as any normal person would have? Shouldn't he have realised that he missed his work?

For once she regretted the high standard of equipment in Alistair's office. It had made her job infinitely easier, and she had marvelled at all the gadgets and computers that kept him in touch with his companies, never once realising that they also managed to enable Conrad to more than keep in touch with his own companies as well.

She finally fell asleep with disgruntled reluctance, and awoke the following morning to a perfectly cloudless, still day. No refreshing breeze, only the sultry heaviness of relentless heat.

Through the opened window the heat was leaden and cloying, and Emma quickly shut the window, switching on the air-conditioning for the first time in days. There was no point getting a headache from the humidity when she needed all her wits about her.

When she got to Alistair's bedroom, it was to find Conrad already there, and in the relaxed attitude of someone who had probably been there for some time.

They both looked at her, Alistair unable to conceal the smug contentment on his face.

'Emma, darling, I've broken the news to Alistair.'

Conrad's eyes darkened as he came towards her, reaching to stroke the side of her face with his fingers. Emma fought down the melting feeling that swept over her, telling herself that it was all a sham and she had better not be foolish enough to forget it, even for one minute.

'Oh, good,' she said, forcing a smile.

'You'll have to do better than that,' Conrad whispered in her ear. 'Don't forget we're not playing games here. Alistair's health is at stake.'

He kissed her on the neck, sending a flood of colour to her face, and then slung his arm over her shoulders.

He drew her along to Alistair's bedside.

'My dear, congratulations.' Alistair beamed at her. 'It's an old man's dream come true. My beloved granddaughter, lost to me for years, now to be married to the young man who's always been as close to me as my own flesh and blood.'

'Not just an old man's dream,' Conrad murmured softly, 'ours too. Isn't that right, darling? I'm only sorry that it took us so long to find out.'

'Right,' Emma muttered, feeling a sickening wave of guilt wash over her. Why had she ever gone along with this damn fool scheme? She tried gracefully to disengage herself from Conrad's arms, but he pulled her tighter towards him. His fingers tangled in her long hair, ensuring that any further attempt to get away from him would be useless.

Talk about playing it to the hilt, she thought with desperation. She made herself relax against him, disturbingly aware of the steady beat of his heart and the warmth of his chest.

'I was telling Conrad a while back, before you came in, that I had hoped you two would hit it off, but when did you realise that you were in love?' Alistair looked interestedly at Emma's flushed face.

She turned to Conrad provocatively, her green eyes gleaming. 'When was it, darling?'

As far as she was concerned, if he was such a good actor, then he could damn well do all the talking. She hadn't liked the scheme from the start and she would leave it to him to carry through as much as she could, even though she reluctantly had to admit that already Alistair was looking better.

'Oh, you explain,' Conrad murmured, stroking her hair but not releasing his grip. 'You women are so much more articulate at these things.'

The bastard, Emma thought, smiling sweetly at Alistair.

'I think I fell in love the minute I laid eyes on him,' she said, speaking with difficulty. In a minute she was going to choke. She only hoped that Conrad had been right, and that the end would justify all this, because right now she felt horribly trapped and deceitful.

His hand slipped to her waist, resting lightly underneath her breasts. She felt her body respond automatically and forced herself to ignore the melting feeling in her legs.

'So did I,' Conrad agreed. 'I didn't realise it at first, but isn't that always the way with true love?'

Emma chose not to reply to his question. She listened numbly while Alistair congratulated them, murmuring vaguely when he began discussing wedding plans.

'You'll make a beautiful bride, Emma,' Alistair beamed at her. 'You'll make up for the shambles over my own daughter's elopement. And you're both so perfectly suited. I could see it from the start.'

Conrad squeezed her waist lovingly and Emma tried not to stiffen. To do what she really wanted to do, which was to sink back into his embrace, would have been dangerous.

When they were finally outside and the door to Alistair's room firmly shut, Emma rounded on him.

'I thought you said that the possibility of Alistair bringing up the question of marriage wouldn't happen. And now that we're out of the bedroom, I'll thank you to keep your hands to yourself!' She stood back from him, impatiently sweeping her hair away from her face.

Conrad obediently stepped back, thrusting both hands into his pockets. 'And I thought that you enjoyed it.'

'Well, you thought wrong!'

'You're the first woman to say that to me.' His mouth was smiling, but the depths of his eyes were serious, and it flitted through Emma's head that he probably was telling the truth. Women for him had been conquered territory the moment he set eyes on them. His lazy sexuality, his power, would draw even the most hardened feminist. Women could not resist the sort of easy self-assurance that he possessed.

'You still haven't answered my question,' she snapped. 'How are we going to get Alistair off the subject of marriage?'

Conrad turned away and began walking slowly down the staircase. Emma hurried behind him.

'Why worry about it?' he asked with what Emma considered overwhelming naïveté. Couldn't he foresee the problems? She could. Now that they had embarked on this, she could foresee hundreds of them. How could he simply adopt such a *laissez-faire* attitude?

He was still striding ahead of her. She stood still and glared at him, her hands on her hips.

'No breakfast?' he called over his shoulder.

'I resent having to trot behind you like your pet dog!' Emma responded on a high note. 'This is serious, so if you wouldn't mind treating it as such...'

'Only on a full stomach.' He vanished towards the kitchen.

Emma's teeth clamped together and she followed him through, helping herself to coffee from the percolator.

'I didn't realise you meant it,' she said sarcastically, eyeing the plateful of fried bacon, sausage and eggs which he was preparing for himself. 'Do you think you have enough calories there, or perhaps you could set the whole thing off by simply melting lard over the lot?'

Through the kitchen window she could see Esther tending to the herb beds, clipping bunches of parsley and thyme which she used liberally in her food.

Conrad sat opposite her and began eating.

'Would you like some?' He gave her a concerned look which didn't fool her for an instant.

'Thanks, but I don't think my blood-pressure could stand it. And you still haven't answered my question.'

'Question?' he asked with polite interest.

'I was saying,' Emma repeated acidly, 'that this little game of yours is already beginning to have flaws. Alistair is talking about marriage as though we'll be walking up the aisle in a few days' time.'

'All the more reason for him to start his recuperating, then.'

As Esther bustled into the kitchen, Conrad stood up and stretched, throwing her a grin and moved to stand behind Emma's chair. He bent over, enfolding her in his arms.

'Congratulations,' Esther said with a broad smile. 'It'll be nice to have a wedding in the family.'

Emma gritted her teeth. She had thought that their little plan was not going to extend beyond Alistair. Clearly she had been wrong.

'I didn't think you knew,' she said lightly, feeling slightly dizzy as Conrad stroked her collarbone, his fingers moving dangerously close to the swell of her breasts.

'Of course, darling.' Conrad kissed her ear. 'Esther's like one of the family. After Alistair, she was the first person I told.'

'Fine. Darling. And when shall we be putting the notice in *The Times*?'

She heard Conrad chuckle.

'So what you two up to today? You want me to prepare lunch for you?' Esther was sifting through the herbs, picking out the best clumps and laying them to one side.

'I don't think so,' Conrad said quickly, silencing Emma's protests that she was going to do some work and then relax in the cove. 'We're going to see something of the island. Maybe you could just cut some sandwiches for us.'

Esther nodded.

Sandwiches? Tours of the island? Emma felt as though her life was suddenly running away from her. In the past she had always been in control. She had friends, went to the theatre, to parties, let men take her out to dinner, but she had always been firmly in the driving seat, in charge of her own life.

She knew where she stood, and she liked that feeling of knowing that she could always extricate herself from any situation that proved difficult.

Now the driving seat had given way to a skateboard and most of the time she didn't even know what direction it was going to take. It was heady, and it was dangerous.

Decisions were swept out of her mouth before she even had the opportunity to utter them. By Conrad—a man whose motives, she constantly had to remind herself, were suspect, to say the least.

His hands were still resting on her shoulders and with a sudden move Emma stood up, relieved when he moved aside to accommodate her.

'Perhaps you should get ready,' he said mildly, his eyes running over her, taking in the curves of her body underneath the fine cotton layer of clothing.

'Can't I go as I am?'

'I suggest you bring a swimsuit. No need to put it on here—you can change into it if you need to.'

Where, Emma thought, in the car? She resolved to put it on the minute she went upstairs. But she would keep on what she was wearing. The heat had not abated;

if anything it was becoming more claustrophobic, and thicker clothes would be unthinkable.

On the spur of the moment she packed a towel and a spare jersey, as well as her book, not that she had much hope of being able to read it. Even if they decided simply to find a beach somewhere, the thought of relaxing enough to enjoy a book with Conrad close by was a joke.

Her mind and body did funny things when he was around. He had a knack of throwing her off-key, although she thought as she looked at the hardback book that it could prove an ideal weapon if he decided to take their pretend engagement too far.

Alistair was delighted when Emma went to tell him what their plans were for the day.

'How very romantic,' he sighed, winking at her. He really was looking better. He had completely relinquished the bed, preferring to sit in his wheelchair by the window.

In fact, he was already talking about starting work again in a couple of days' time.

'It'll mean so much more now,' he informed her. 'I shall have to do some rethinking.'

'Why?' Emma asked ingenuously.

'To fit you in, of course. My granddaughter is part of my life, even though I missed out on a few years at the beginning. I want to incorporate all that's happened in these past few weeks into my autobiography. It's far more meaningful to me than all the wealth I've managed to accumulate over the years.'

Emma couldn't argue the point. She was just glad that her grandfather looked so well. Robust, even.

She was more than prepared to stay and marvel on his recovery with him, when the alternative was Conrad's company, but Alistair was having none of it. He shooed her towards the door, and seemed to be, she noticed disgruntledly, far more excited about the prospect of her touring the island with Conrad than she was.

'Are you sure you'll be all right here on your own for the whole day?' she asked as a last resort, not surprised when he threw aside her remark with a nonchalant wave of his hand.

'Esther's here,' he reminded her. 'So off you go.'

Conrad was waiting for her by the car, wearing a pair of denim shorts and a blue and white striped jersey. A picnic hamper had been packed for them by Esther, which, Conrad informed her as they were settled in the car, contained enough food to feed an army.

Emma laughed nervously and asked where they were going. She was already beginning to feel apprehensive at the thought of being isolated with him for several hours.

Outside the heat sat around them heavily, unrelieved by even the slightest hint of a breeze. The few people they passed, the animals, all seemed to be moving in sluggish slow motion.

They drove past a roadside stall, a makeshift affair of wooden boards groaning under the weight of fruit, all stacked into neat piles, and Emma was amused to see that the boy in charge was sound asleep in a hammock nearby. At least, she thought, she wasn't the only one affected by the thick, gluey heat today.

'I've decided to take us sailing,' Conrad said, half turning to see her reaction.

Emma received this doubtfully. 'I don't know how to sail,' she pointed out. 'In fact, I've only been on a sailing boat twice in my lifetime, and both times were disastrous. Maybe we could just go for a quick outing to Pigeon Point.'

She stressed the word quick, hoping that he would take the hint, which he didn't.

'I won't be of any help to you at all,' she persisted.

'It's not really a sailing boat, more of a small cabin cruiser. Just big enough for about four people, with two rooms, which should give us some protection from this sun. We can anchor out at sea and do some swimming.'

'Four people?' Emma asked hopefully. 'Will we have company?'

'Oh, no,' Conrad mocked. 'We are, after all, desperately in love and in no need of anyone else's company.' He began humming under his breath and Emma lapsed into silence, staring outside at the scorching countryside. Even the coconut trees seemed to be drooping, their heads hanging towards the earth.

Next to her, Conrad manoeuvred the car with precision to Store Bay, where their boat was waiting for them.

The sea was flat and calm and the sky perfectly cloudless. Emma climbed aboard before Conrad could help her up, determined to keep any physical contact between them to a minimum and for appearances only when Alistair was around.

The boat was exactly as Conrad had described: small, with a sheltered cabin area just large enough for two people, definitely a squeeze should there have been four.

'I hope you know how to handle one of these,' she said to him as he finished paying the boat owner and leapt on board.

'Don't you have any faith in me? Believe me, I've handled them more than once.'

'In similar circumstances, I suppose?' Emma threw at him, realising too late that she sounded at the very least childish, and at the very worst jealous.

'With women, yes, if that's what you mean.' He glanced at her as the engine throbbed into life and he began steering away from the shoreline.

'I meant with passengers on board,' Emma lied, scarlet. As the boat gathered speed, the salt air whipped her hair across her face and she fished an elastic band out of her pocket, carelessly tying it into a ponytail at the back.

'Leave it out.'

'What?'

'Your hair—leave it out. It looks sexier.'

Emma stared at him, her mouth suddenly dry. The shoreline was fast becoming a thin strip in the distance, and the realisation that soon she would be miles away from land, miles away from any escape route, hit her like a thunderbolt.

'I prefer it like this,' she told him warily, raising her voice to drown the sound of the motor. She turned away to put some distance between them and felt his hand from behind. Before she could protest he had pulled the elastic band from her hair and tossed it into the churning water.

'That's better.'

Better for whom? she thought. She retreated to the deck, cautiously peeled off her clothes down to her bikini, and sat down on her towel. When there was nothing around them but ocean she felt the boat slowing down and finally stopping.

This, she thought, was a bad idea. Conrad was easing himself to join her and she watched him surreptitiously, taking in his quick, lithe movements as he tossed the anchor overboard.

'Amazing, isn't it?' he asked, gesturing to the never-ending stretch of water. 'Doesn't it make you feel insignificant?'

Emma nodded slowly. He was right, of course. They were no more than specks on the horizon. The solitude in the immense wilderness of sea around them was formidable.

The heat was sapping. They chatted lazily about any number of things, half drowsy in the intense warmth. When Conrad stood up and asked her whether she was going to join him for a swim, Emma peered dubiously down at the water.

'It doesn't look very inviting,' she said, looking at the black depths. 'Anything could be underneath there waiting for us to jump in.'

Conrad laughed, 'Anything like what? And what makes you think that they're waiting for us? Don't you think that they've got better things to do than wait around for a couple of nondescript human beings to jump in the water for a swim?' He stretched out his hand for her and Emma grabbed hold of it, pulling herself up.

Immediately she was on her feet, she released him and went over to the side of the boat, watching in fascinated admiration as Conrad dived cleanly into the water, disappearing and resurfacing a minute later.

Did nothing frighten him? True, he was a strong swimmer, she had seen ample evidence of that, but this was different. The water was not transparent and blue but dark and deep and ominously still.

'Don't be such a coward!' he called, floating on his back with his feet crossed. 'Don't you ever take risks?'

There was enough of a taunt in his voice for Emma to throw caution to the winds and plunge into the water, gasping at the first cold impact. She swam over to Conrad, feeling peculiarly safe with him close to her. She had no idea why, since he could hardly fend off a school of sharks, or even one for that matter.

'What about sharks?' she asked in a low voice, glancing around her cautiously.

'What about them?'

'Are there any?'

He looked around, a wry smile curving his lips. 'None that I can see just at the moment. Don't worry, I'll keep my eyes open, and the minute I spot a wayward fin I'll let you know.'

'You know what I mean,' Emma accused him lightly, liking him more than she wanted to admit, in this teasing, easy mood, finding it too easy to forget that he should inspire caution and not camaraderie, 'Sharks like warm water. There are bound to be a few, somewhere around us.'

'True,' Conrad agreed. 'But we'll just have to gamble that they can find more interesting things to do than attack us.'

'Mr Fearless,' Emma mocked, grinning.

He smiled back at her, his eyes darkening, and Emma swam away, circling the boat, her confidence increasing as she realised that she was as safe here as she would be crossing a busy street in London. Safer, probably.

By the time they climbed back on to the boat she was surprised to find that she was really enjoying herself. A few clouds were gathering on the horizon, but there was still no relief from the heat. It enveloped her the minute she was back on the deck, drying off her body in a matter of seconds, before she even had time to rub herself down with her towel.

They unpacked Esther's hamper in the shelter of the cabin, spreading the food out on the little table. There was crab, roast beef and chicken sandwiches, a potato salad, lots of tomatoes and a Thermos of coffee.

'And of course,' Conrad produced from the bottom of the basket, 'this.'

'Wine?' Emma laughed, 'Esther packed that?'

'No. That, I must confess, was entirely my own doing.'

Their eyes met and Emma looked away quickly, busying herself with the food, neatly serving out the sandwiches and salad on to paper plates.

The first warning they had of the storm was a sharp crack of thunder, as clear and as unexpected as the sound of a gunshot, and she heard Conrad swear under his breath. He left the cabin and returned seconds later wearing a grim expression.

Emma was standing at the tiny cabin window, staring at the rolling black clouds which seemed to be gathering momentum by the second.

'I should have known,' he muttered forcefully.

'Known? Known what?'

'Take a look outside.'

'I have. It's going to rain. We can always head back now in time.' She hastily began stacking the left-over food back into the basket.

'I can see you have no experience whatsoever of the tropics,' Conrad said cynically, 'Rain over here isn't like a downpour in England. And this isn't just going to be a light shower, over in fifteen minutes. We're in for something more severe than that. I should have known. All the signs were there. The heaviness in the air, the stillness. I asked that damned man who rented us the boat about it, but he said that there was nothing to worry about. The hurricane had swept through some of the islands further north, but Tobago was safe.'

Emma had gone white. 'What are we going to do?'

'Ride it through, what else?'

There was another crack of thunder and the stillness was replaced by a sudden, cool wind, churning the waters into a choppy black mass.

'But it was so sunny a minute ago.' She had instinctively edged closer to Conrad and slipped on her clothes.

'That's the nature of the beast,' he said drily, cramming anything that could move under the seat and securing them as fast as he could. 'The weather over here can change in a matter of seconds.'

As though to prove his point, the wind gathered force, gently buffeting the tiny cabin cruiser against the water.

'Where are you going?' Emma asked desperately, as Conrad prepared to go outside.

'I'll have to try and steer the boat into the waves.' He grimaced. 'Stay calm, whatever you do. The last thing I need is a hysterical female.' Before she could reply, he lowered his head, and she felt his lips brush against hers, then he was gone, and Emma retreated to the window, to a view of rain slashing against the water in a dense, black sheet, and to the wind driving the water into a frenzied, seething mass.

Conrad had been right. She had no experience of weather like this. In England there was always a prolonged, polite warning of rain or snow. Here nature extended no such civilities. She released the full brunt of her displeasure with impressive speed.

Emma huddled against a wooden support, grasping it with one hand as the boat rocked furiously, like a matchbox tossed into rapids.

Every few minutes a gush of water would drench the window, blocking her view. She wanted desperately to go and see how Conrad was faring, but she knew without doubt that the last thing he needed was her presence behind the steering-wheel.

Hadn't he said so to her? No hysterical woman. She traced her lips where he had lightly kissed her, and tried to staunch the sudden, fierce need she felt for him, and the painful knowledge that what he was doing was necessary but highly dangerous.

Outside, the skies were black, as though night had prematurely fallen, even though it was only just two in the afternoon.

What if something happened to Conrad? Her blood froze as she considered the possibility. She had admitted her physical attraction to him, had argued that whatever she felt stopped there. It had to stop there because it would have been sheer folly for it to progress any further.

She was not his type, and anyway she couldn't trust him as far as she could throw him. That knowledge, bitter though it was, was her protection.

So why couldn't she simply follow the path pointed out to her by her head?

There was another roll of thunder and Emma covered her ears with her hands. If Conrad could ride out this storm, then she could ride out whatever it was that was slowly gnawing away at her insides.

Wasn't it all a question of time?

CHAPTER EIGHT

EMMA had no idea how much time had passed before the fierce pounding of the boat against the waves became more of a steady roll, and the wind gradually began to die away.

The rain was still falling heavily, but on to calmer waters. Emma stretched her legs, wincing in pain as she rested her weight on to her stiffened joints.

The first thought in her head was to check Conrad, to make sure that everything was all right. She balanced herself against the wooden side of the cabin, walking unsteadily towards the door when a sudden jolt sent her flying across the floor, crashing ungracefully against one of the benches.

She yelped in agony as an arrow of pain shot through her ankle. Gently she massaged the foot, hoping that nothing was broken. A sound from the cabin door made her raise her head and she saw Conrad framed against the grey sky, dripping wet.

A rush of relief swept over her, as powerful as anything she had felt before. She stared up at him, unable to speak, hardly able to think, simply ridiculously grateful that he was in one piece. She had a sudden chill of horror as she realised what might have happened to him out there. He could, for starters, have been swept out to sea. In violent weather like this, it wasn't an impossibility. If he had been, he would have vanished without a trace.

She felt her throat constrict and looked down hurriedly.

'I heard a noise,' he said, coming across to where she was still sitting on the floor.

'It's my ankle,' Emma said gruffly. 'I was trying to get outside and I fell.'

Conrad looked at her white face incredulously. 'Trying to get outside? What for? Did you think that you could help steer us to safety?'

Emma felt the prick of tears behind her eyes and swallowed painfully. 'Thanks for the sympathy!'

'Let me have a look,' he commanded, reaching out towards her.

'I'll be fine.'

'Dammit, Emma. This is no time for childish heroics. Let me see your ankle! Now!'

Reluctantly she stretched her leg out, biting her lip as his fingers pressed against her ankle, delicately trying to determine the seriousness of her fall.

'Sorry I tore into you like that,' he muttered, his head bent as he inspected her foot. 'It's been nightmarish out there for the past two hours, but thankfully we're out of the worst.'

'Two hours!'

'I told you it wouldn't be a fifteen-minute downpour. I'll need your T-shirt.'

'What for?' she asked, feeling embarrassingly undressed as she pulled the jersey over her head, even though her bikini top covered her.

Without answering, Conrad tore it into one long strip.

'What do you think you're doing?' She stood up, falling back in pain as her foot crumpled from under her.

'What does it look like? I'm doing my best to make a bandage for this ankle. I can hardly use my shirt, it's soaking wet. Looks like a sprain; I can't feel any broken bones.'

He carefully began to wind the cloth around her foot until the ankle was securely bandaged. 'Damn fool thing to have done,' he commented neutrally.

'Believe me, it wasn't premeditated! I don't normally hurl myself around boats on the offchance that I might break my ankle!' How could she have ever felt tearful relief that this man was back in the cabin with her?

She watched as he stripped to the waist and sat next to her.

'I've anchored the boat. The wind's gone, but it'll continue raining for at least another hour and there's no point our even thinking about making it back until it clears a bit more.'

'Alistair will be worried.'

'There's not much I can do about that. There's no radio transmitter on this boat, so we're uncontactable.'

Emma digested this information in silence.

He looked, she conceded sympathetically, tired. The wind and rain had whipped his black hair around his face, giving him a swarthy, unkempt appearance. In another era, she thought, he would have made a great pirate.

He gesticulated to the bottle of wine and Emma shook her head in refusal. The last thing she needed was alcohol, and he apparently agreed, pouring himself some coffee instead, which he swallowed in one quick gulp.

They hadn't spoken, and the bleakness outside, pressing on the small panes of glass, seemed to magnify the atmosphere of intimacy that descended on them.

When he beckoned her to sit next to him, she found herself complying.

Of course, it wouldn't do to forget that she was in dangerous waters, both outside and in; that they were only pretending to be engaged for Alistair's benefit and that Conrad couldn't give two hoots for her outside that. Even so...

The sea had calmed considerably. Only the occasional gust of wind shook the little cruiser as if to remind them that they could shelve any thought of heading back to land for the time being.

'Don't worry. It's over,' Conrad murmured soothingly. He placed an arm around her shoulder and Emma leant against it, liking the warm, safe feeling that it gave her.

'Was it very bad up there?'

'I've spent more enjoyable afternoons, but fortunately I didn't have time to be afraid. When you're caught up in a situation like that, there's no room for fear.'

'Are you ever afraid?' Emma asked curiously. 'Of anything?'

'Oh, yes,' he said softly, 'but not what you'd expect.' He gave a short laugh, but didn't elaborate.

Instead, he looked down at her, his blue eyes warm, too warm for comfort. She really shouldn't be sprawled against him the way she was. She shifted slightly, and Conrad's arm curled further around her, so that his hand was right by her mouth.

She looked at it, seeing the way the dark hairs were silky-smooth on his wrist, the hands strong and not at all like a businessman's manicured hands.

She found herself raising her own to take it, linking her fingers through his. He stiffened slightly, then relaxed, and she felt his warmth infuse her like a heady fix.

She settled more comfortably. Her hair swept down across her face and she flicked it aside.

'I knew I should have tied it back.'

Conrad didn't answer. Instead he entwined his fingers in the long, tumbling mass, looping it around his fingers.

Outside, the rain continued to beat against the grimy window in the cabin, but inside the silence was deafening. A cold, sober awareness rushed over Emma, but she shut her mind to it, closing her eyes to enjoy the sensation of Conrad's fingers lightly stroking her hair.

'You're very tempting,' he murmured, and the look in his eyes made her nerves tingle with excitement.

She knew that she ought to protest, she half opened her mouth and he lowered his head to hers, his lips brushing over her upturned face. Emma could feel her whole body yearning for him with a desire over which she had lost control.

She smiled and moaned softly, her body shifting closer to his.

'I can smell the salt and the sea on you,' Conrad muttered unevenly, and he stretched out his arm so that her head was resting against it.

'It's as if I'm drunk with you,' he whispered against her neck. 'Do you feel the same way? Tell me you want me as badly as I want you.' She could see feverish passion in his eyes as he looked down at her and she felt herself drowning in it.

Oh, yes, she was drunk with him as well, intoxicated by the feel of him. She knew well enough what she was doing, but was powerless to stop. Everything in her, all of her cool, analytical practicality, was crumbling under the impact of the restless emotions surging through her.

She heard herself responding to him, telling him what he wanted to hear and what she felt, telling him that she wanted him. It was madness, but a delicious, persuasive madness, a delirium that filled her every nerve.

Conrad sighed heavily.

'You're the most provocative, stubborn woman I have ever met.' The words were muffled as his lips trailed across her neck.

Emma arched back, curling her hands in his hair, guiding his mouth to hers.

He kissed her with deepening force, his tongue exploring her mouth, and Emma responded with trembling hunger. She had fought so long against this, knowing that if she gave in again to him she would be lost, and she was. She didn't care. She was filled with a driving, suffocating need for him and all she wanted was to succumb to it.

His hands moved across her stomach and her nipples hardened to meet his touch. His mouth, demanding, explored her breasts, and Emma shivered weakly. Tentatively she slipped her fingers underneath the elastic waistband of his trunks, feeling the hard curve of his buttocks under her hand.

Her face felt hot and flushed, as though she were gripped by a raging fever.

His movements now were urgent, his body covered in a fine film of perspiration to match her own. He gently eased her out of her shorts, murmuring as he caressed her naked thighs.

Restlessly he pulled her free of the remnants of her clothing. As he raised himself to strip, Emma stared at his hard body with greedy concentration, dwelling on the firm lines of his body, the fine dark hairs that spiralled down from his navel.

'Tell me you want me, Emma,' he commanded shakily, lowering his body against hers.

Emma stared drowsily at him, 'You know I do. More than anything.' With a fierceness, she thought, that engulfed her.

She felt a sharp stab as he thrust against her, and with her eyes closed did not realise that he was staring down at her in surprise. Her hands gripped his hips, pulling him to her.

'Emma,' he said huskily.

'I know. Please.' She lay back, her body suffused with mounting passion, moving with instinctive rhythm to him, plumbing the depths of a desire which she did not know existed.

The grey sheet of rain was fading away. Through the cabin window, she could actually see patches of blue sky struggling to peep through the dense pillows of black clouds. They lay back next to each other, Emma still in the crook of his arm.

'Silly, isn't it,' she said, more to herself than to Conrad, 'a virgin at my age?'

'Not silly at all. Rather special, in fact.' He seemed wrapped up in his own thoughts, and as Emma watched his face, resisting the urge to reach out and caress it, she could feel the first drops of cold reality begin to trickle over her, just as the sun began filtering into the cabin.

Of course, he didn't love her. He had made love to her because he fancied her, and because both their defences had been lowered. He had acted on instinct, touching her in a way that had left no room for doubt in her mind.

Not then, anyway. Now, the doubts which had been pushed to one side were becoming a steady, cold stream.

Why had he made love to her? He wanted her. She had felt it in his urgent moans as he thrust against her. But maybe there was more to it than that.

She looked at the handsome, clever face, a face designed to have its own way with the female sex.

He could have anyone he wanted, she thought. As Sophia said, he was the biggest and brightest catch in the ocean. So why her? Unless, a tiny insistent voice said, she had what he wanted. Namely, money.

Did he think that she was in line for Alistair's inheritance? Had that made her irresistible?

The palms of her hands were clammy and her head was spinning. All those thoughts rushing through her mind, gathering momentum even as she tried to banish them.

She groaned inwardly, hating him and hating herself even more because, despite everything, she had wanted him. She had needed him to touch her, like some fairy-tale Sleeping Beauty waiting for that single kiss that would revive her.

Except, she thought miserably, this was no fairy-tale. If it were, then she would be able to at least gather her self-possession, and walk away from him with some dignity. But now she realised with horror that the attraction which she had labelled her private, physical obsession for him was much more than that. Perhaps that was how it had started. A tingling in her veins whenever he was near, the knowledge that he had managed to do what no one else had ever done, which was somehow to get under her skin until he filled her whole body and mind with his presence.

Oh, no, she was in love with him. All his little habits and expressions rushed over her, bombarding her with their profuseness. She had not realised just how much she had been taking in, details which she had stored away and which their act of lovemaking now released.

She drew away from him sharply, fumbling to get on her clothes with frantic, trembling hands. When he pulled her back against him, she looked at him with alarm and tugged away. How could she? How could she have made love to a man who cared nothing for her, and who quite probably had used her for his own ends? He was quite an expert at using people, she had seen that for herself.

He had used Sophia, hadn't he? He had been more than prepared to marry someone simply because it suited him, and he had made love to her for the same reason.

'What's the matter?' he asked lazily, making no effort to dress.

Emma grabbed his clothes and threw them on him.

'I think you should get dressed,' she said coldly, averting her eyes.

'You do, do you?' He stood up, his face clenched and hard. 'Don't you think it's a bit late to be putting on this puritan act?' He forced her to face him, and she controlled the pounding in her head, staring into his bright, glittering eyes with contempt.

'And you can wipe that expression off your face,' he said tightly.

'I'll look at you the way I want.'

He slipped back on his clothes, still soaking wet from the rain.

'You weren't looking at me like that a minute ago. Why the sudden change?'

'Has the weather cleared enough for us to leave?'

'Answer me, damn you!' He gripped her by her hair and Emma winced in pain.

'I want you to get this boat going. Now!'

'I asked you a question!'

'And when you ask a question,' she jeered, 'you get an answer, right? Just as you get whatever you want, right? Including women!'

'Right.'

'Well, not with me!' she shouted. He had released her, and she backed against the side of the cabin, until she was pressed against it and couldn't move any further back.

'Really? Are you going to try and convince me that I forced you to make love with me?'

'I don't have to try and convince you of anything!' Just as I don't have to answer your questions!'

The watery sun caught his hair and she looked away. It hurt too much to continue staring at him. It was like a test of strength, trying to fight against the insane love that she felt for him.

'You'll damn well talk to me, or else we'll stay right here for the rest of the evening, and longer if we have to!'

'Is that some kind of threat?'

'You're damn right, lady.'

He moved across to her, and her body froze as he placed his hands on either side of her, making any escape impossible.

'When all else fails, do you normally resort to threats?' she asked scornfully.

'No. Believe me, this is a first! I don't normally make love, only to find that the first thing my woman wants to do is get out as quickly as she can!'

'I'm not your woman.'

'You were, not too long ago.'

'Only in the physical sense!'

He had left off his shirt, and the compulsion to place her hands on the flat, firm planes of his torso was so strong that she stuck them safely behind her back.

Why hadn't she listened to reason? Reason had told her from the very beginning to steer clear of him. If she had, she would never have fallen in love with him, and would never have found herself in the mess she was in.

'So what is it, then? Is it because you were a virgin? That's no reason to feel ashamed, you know. Just the opposite.'

A slow red flush crept up her cheeks.

'That's not the reason,' she said in a hard voice. 'If you want answers, then here they are. We should never have made love; it was a mistake. I think that I was just so relieved when you came through that door, so relieved that everything was going to be all right, that I gave in to some kind of temporary insanity.'

'In other words, let's just blame it on the heat of the moment.'

'That's right,' she said expressionlessly.

He didn't answer. He turned away, and when he faced her again it was to inform her that the journey back would probably only take forty minutes to an hour, and the sooner they got going, the better.

She watched him disappear through the cabin door, and then she collapsed heavily on one of the wooden benches, like a puppet whose strings had been suddenly cut.

Why dwell on what had happened? She had given in to him without restraint, she had ignored all the alarm bells sounding in her head.

She had swept all her suspicions tidily under the carpet, because, in the grip of her shaking passion, it had been simply more convenient to have them there, out of the way.

But, worse than all that, worse than her loss of control, her shameful, eager responses, was that she had fallen in love with him.

It did not bear thinking about.

She began tidying the cabin as quickly as she could, moving about slowly with her bandaged ankle.

She could feel the boat gathering speed, and reluctantly she made her way outside to the deck, joining him behind the steering-wheel, watching his hands with an inward shudder as she remembered how he had touched her, and politely made conversation about the journey back.

Conrad answered her questions with remote abstraction, barely acknowledging her presence.

She abandoned all attempt at conversation on the drive back, which they made in silence.

When they arrived back at the house, Esther was waiting for them by the front door, her face anxious and worried. She insisted that they go and see Alistair before changing, to put his mind at rest.

'He's been imagining the worst,' she confided, and Emma half smiled, thinking that the worst had happened, but not in the context that Esther meant.

Alistair was overjoyed to see them. He told them that they should really change into drier clothes, and then promptly insisted that they describe in detail what it had been like in the storm.

Conrad obligingly filled in the details, standing by the window with his arms folded, glancing perfunctorily at

Emma when she chipped in with some remark of her own.

If Alistair noticed the coolness between them, he showed no sign of it. As they were leaving the room, Conrad slipped his arm over her shoulders, and she remembered with a stab of pain that they were supposed to be engaged. The loving couple. The situation was painfully farcical.

She forced the muscles of her face to smile at Alistair, looking away before he could see that the smile did not reach her eyes. He was shrewd enough to notice something like that, and whatever happened between herself and Conrad she would not jeopardise Alistair's visible recovery by aborting the charade, much as she wanted to. For better or for worse, they had embarked on this and she was quite determined to see it through to the end.

Once Alistair was better, and that looked to be sooner rather than later, she would leave the island.

As soon as they were outside the door, she shrugged Conrad's arm away from her.

'There's no one out here to impress,' she said coldly, tilting her chin upwards.

'Quite right,' Conrad came back quickly. 'There's no need to point out the obvious.'

She saw something flash through his eyes, something that she couldn't decipher, and immediately came to the conclusion that it was antipathy.

'Another thing,' she persevered. 'Alistair has more or less recovered. He's even talking about starting work tomorrow.'

'And you're wondering when we can call off this little game of ours,' Conrad finished for her.

'Yes.'

'We can break it to him within the next few days. I see no reason to prolong this.'

'Fine. That suits me perfectly.'

She swung round and began trotting down the stairs. The sharp staccato of his voice had cut her to the quick, but she would not let him see it.

She spent the remainder of the day cloistered in the study, preparing for work the following day, and returned there early the next morning. When the phone rang soon after lunch, which she'd had sent in, she almost ignored it, knowing that there was a good chance it would be for Conrad, and she did not want to have to go and look for him, and see that cold cynicism stamped on his face.

As it turned out it was Lloyd on the other end, over in Tobago because, he said, he could not get her out of his mind.

'Really?' Emma remarked drily. 'Now why do I find that a little difficult to believe?'

'Well, it could have been the truth. Actually, I have to see someone over here about some lighting equipment for the nightclub, but I also couldn't get you out of my mind.'

Emma laughed shortly, thinking how sweet those words would have sounded had they been uttered by someone else, in a different situation.

Still, it was nice hearing from Lloyd. His bantering lightened her mood, and when he suggested coming over for dinner Emma greeted the suggestion with enthusiasm. She had been dreading the ordeal of dinner alone with Conrad, if indeed he chose to make an appearance. Lloyd, at least, would do away with the necessity of even talking to Conrad, if she didn't want to.

'Eight all right?' he asked.

'The sooner, the better,' Emma responded fervently.

When evening came she took her time dressing, choosing a pale green dress which made her eyes gleam like emeralds and showed off her tan which, she thought, would be the envy of her friends back home. When she returned to England.

She made it down the stairs just in time to see Lloyd's car sweeping up the driveway. As she threw open the front door she was greeted with blaring pop music that was cut off abruptly when the engine was switched off.

Lloyd enfolded her in his arms and then presented her with a bouquet of flowers which, he claimed, had been picked with his own fair hands.

She laughed, smelling the delicate blossoms and thinking that it was almost a shame that they had been picked at all. The wild, exotic flowers over here only seemed truly beautiful when they were nestled in their natural foliage. To see them in a vase was somewhat similar to seeing a lion caged at the zoo.

Lloyd was already regaling her with all the things which she had been missing out on by being in Tobago, instead of accepting his invitation to visit him in Trinidad. He stared at her in amazement when she began telling him about the storm, which, he informed her, had swept through Trinidad and had found him well and truly ensconced in his flat.

'A coward has a thousand lives, or something like that,' he grinned, 'Where's the lord of the manor, then?' He glanced around and Emma shrugged.

'Maybe his experiences in the boat have taken their toll and he's cooped up in bed with delayed shock.'

'I doubt that,' Emma commented cynically. 'If anything, he enjoyed the whole thing.'

She diverted the conversation, not wanting to discuss Conrad, and unsure as to whether she should mention her make-believe engagement. In the end she decided against it. It was much too involved, and would be over in a day or two anyway.

Over dinner, she let Lloyd set the conversation and they spent the evening discussing movies and records. She only half listened to what he was saying, however. At times she would find her concentration wandering altogether, and would have to pull herself up to control the crazy urge to look out for Conrad.

She had managed to project a suitable attitude of coldness towards him, but her mind was a little harder to control. It stubbornly continued to bombard her with sharp, strong images of him which made her blush. She never would have believed that she could close her eyes and feel a rush of sensation, but in the privacy of her bedroom the image of him was so strong that she could almost reach out and touch him. She closed her eyes, and could smell him, see the way his eyes crinkled when he laughed with genuine amusement.

When he finally did make an appearance, it was to find them settled comfortably on the sofa in the sitting-room, sipping coffee, and in Lloyd's case a glass of brandy.

Emma had switched on the stereo, and they were listening to a piece of classical music, which, she had informed Lloyd, would make a change from the pop music which he played every night in his club.

'Besides,' she had added, seeing him make a moue, 'there's not much choice. It's either this, or the pleasant sounds of nothing.'

She had hoped that Lloyd's company would put her in a more relaxed frame of mind, and she had been right. Lloyd did not burden himself with too many worries, not if he could avoid it, and he was blind to other people's worries as well. He was a free spirit and just exactly what Emma needed in the sort of mood that she was in.

Conrad stood at the door, the top buttons of his shirt undone, his hair tousled as though he had just stepped out of bed and had not been bothered to comb it.

Emma raised startled eyes to his.

'We wondered where you had got to,' Lloyd opened jovially.

Conrad walked slowly into the room, and Emma realised with shock that he had been drinking. As he stepped into the light, she could see that he had not shaved and a dark shadow of stubble roughened his face.

'Have you, now?' Conrad muttered through gritted teeth, his eyes not leaving Emma's face.

Lloyd shifted uneasily on the sofa and glanced across at Emma.

'Care to join us in a cup of coffee?' he persevered nervously. 'Or maybe in your case something stronger? The old boy may not have much by way of pop music, but he keeps a comprehensive line in alcohol. You look as if you need it.'

'Really,' Conrad snarled, turning to face him. 'How very observant of you. You clearly missed your calling. You should join the local detective force instead of doing whatever it is you do.'

'Nightclubbing.'

'Oh, yes. Forgot. Nightclubbing.' He dropped each word individually and with contempt.

Emma's initial shock gave way to a rush of anger. How dared he stride into the room and begin insulting her and her guest, who had done nothing to him?

He moved across to the stereo and picked up the Mozart album cover, staring at the record revolving on the turntable.

'Getting in the right mood?' he asked Lloyd sarcastically, then he spun round to Emma, his lips twisted in a sneer. 'I'm surprised you haven't gone the whole hog and dimmed the lights as well. Or did you think that that was just a little bit too passé? Still, I see you've dressed for the occasion.' He ran his eyes slowly over her, from her burning face to the tips of her feet, then back again to her face. 'No? Don't tell me, you always dress like that for dinner with a friend? Right?' He gave a mimicry of a laugh, running his fingers through his black hair.

Emma rounded on him. 'If you have a problem, then I wish you'd go and sort it out somewhere else!' she bit out. 'We'd been having a very pleasant time until you arrived on the scene.'

'Oh, I'm sure you had.'

Lloyd cleared his throat. 'Listen, old chap, why don't you go to bed and sleep it off? You'll feel much better for it in the morning.'

'Yes,' Emma rejoined sweetly, 'why don't you disappear upstairs and sleep it off?' And I hope, she added silently, you feel anything but better in the morning.

'And leave you two down here?' Conrad looked at her with an expression of incredulity. 'Now that wouldn't be very polite of me, would it?'

'I think I can live with that.' The atmosphere between them was electric. Part of her felt very sorry for poor Lloyd, caught up in their private battle of wills, but it didn't manage to quell the anger inside her.

'No, I don't intend going anywhere. I may be many things, but I'm not impolite.' Conrad sat down heavily in between Lloyd and Emma, and folded his arms in the attitude of someone who had no intention of moving. His leg rested against Emma's and she shifted her position to avoid the contact.

Even in the state that he was in, and with her determination to treat him as part of the furniture, she still could not prevent herself from responding to him.

'Maybe I ought to leave,' Lloyd volunteered, gulping down the rest of his brandy and grimacing.

'Maybe you should,' Emma agreed, glaring at Conrad, who had a satisfied little smile playing on his lips.

She rose to see him out, and Conrad stood up as well.

'There's no need to see us to the door,' she said coldly. 'I know how to find my way there.'

'No bother.'

The three of them walked out in an uncomfortable silence. When they were at the front door, Lloyd turned to Emma and said in a low voice, 'It's been a nice evening.' His eyes flickered across to Conrad and then back to her. 'You know that my invitation for you to come and stay with me in Trinidad still stands. Any time. You're a good friend and I'd love to see you.'

'You might see me sooner than you expect.' Over her shoulder she could feel Conrad hovering, listening to every word that they were saying.

If he weren't a rich industrialist, Emma thought, he'd probably be a thug. He certainly had the makings of one, from the athletic, aggressive body to the air of threat that he could create whenever it suited him. It suited him now, and Lloyd almost ran to his car, only turning to wave at Emma when he was secure behind a locked door.

'Well, I hope you're satisfied!' Emma turned on Conrad, fighting to preserve some modicum of self-restraint.

'Very.' He leant against the door-frame and smiled.

'You ruined my evening!'

'So sorry.' He didn't sound in the least bit sorry. In fact, he sounded extremely smug.

'How much have you had to drink anyway?' Emma asked, walking back into the sitting-room to collect the dirty cups and glasses.

'Nothing.' He followed her, and she could almost feel his warm breath on her neck as she stacked the cups and saucers, balancing them precariously in one hand.

He made her edgy. She wished that he would just go to bed. In fact, she wished that he would just leave the island. He had managed to wreck her life and she needed to be a million miles away from him before she could start piecing it together again.

Instead here he was on her heels, watching as she dumped the dirty dishes in the kitchen sink.

'I think I'll go to bed now,' she said flatly, spinning round to find him standing much closer to her than she had expected. He stepped forward and she stepped back. It would have been amusing if her heart weren't doing nervous little somersaults in her chest.

'I wish that twerp wouldn't keep throwing himself at you.' Conrad was staring at her intently, refusing to step aside and let her pass him.

'Lloyd isn't a twerp.'

'He doesn't have a brain in his body.'

'He runs a nightclub! He can't be that brainless!'

'His partner runs the nightclub. Lloyd provides pretty backing; he doesn't actually make any decisions.'

'I'm not going to stand here discussing Lloyd with you,' Emma said coldly, hoping that he couldn't hear her heart thumping heavily in her chest.

'The most responsible decisions Lloyd makes,' Conrad continued as if he hadn't heard her, 'are what colour shirt he's going to put on in the morning. Does this blue shirt match OK with these checked grey socks? Should he go for the Paisley tie or the striped one?'

Emma didn't say anything. She couldn't deny that Lloyd didn't care overmuch for the grittier side of reality, that applying himself to anything serious would be anathema to him, and it infuriated her that Conrad was pointing out the truth, but in the most cynical way possible.

'I can't imagine what you see in him. Is it because he's pushy?'

'He's not pushy,' Emma defended Lloyd stoutly. 'I wanted to see him this evening, or else he would never have come. Not that it's any of your business, but he was over here for a couple of days and he got in touch. I invited him over to dinner.'

Not quite true, but it was plausible enough.

'Is that a fact?' Conrad caught her by the wrist, pinning her to the spot. He wasn't drunk. She could see that now. He was stone-cold sober, and she could also see that he was holding on to his self-control with difficulty. In the sort of mood he was in, she didn't trust him.

She tried to tug her hand away and instead Conrad pulled her towards him so that her body was pressed against his. She could almost feel his heart beating under the fine cotton material of his shirt.

She twisted in panic.

'So,' Conrad rasped. 'You invited him here, did you?'

CHAPTER NINE

EMMA felt her skin tingle with alarm.

'Yes,' she muttered stubbornly, in answer to his question.

He was towering over her, his dark face alarmingly menacing. She knew that the best thing to do would be to try and laugh her way out of the situation, although, eyeing him from under her lashes, she wondered whether a forced humour might have just the opposite effect.

'Well, if he has any thoughts of trying on his juvenile charm with you, he'd better have a rethink.'

The unsteady smile died on her lips. She felt the blood rush to her hairline.

'Or else what?' she nearly shouted. 'I can do precisely as I please, and with whom. You may have made love to me but that's as far as it goes. I've already told you that it was a huge mistake anyway! Whatever I choose to do now is none of your business whatsoever.'

'I'm making it my business,' Conrad hissed, his hand tightening on her so that she winced in pain.

'You're hurting me!'

He slackened his grip, and she felt the blood flow back into her veins.

'You can forget about going to Trinidad to visit him,' he said in a low, harsh voice.

It was on the tip of her tongue to tell him that she had no intention of visiting him, but she bit back the words. Let him think the worst. Did she care? He had no right to act the tyrant with her.

'I'll do exactly as I please,' she said, enunciating every syllable with cold precision. 'If you must know, I was thinking about flying out some time over the weekend.'

She wasn't, but that didn't matter. What mattered was her need to assert her will.

'Not if I have any say in it.'

Emma's green eyes blazed. 'Stop trying to run my life for me! Not only do you have me deceiving my grandfather, but now you're trying to dictate who I see and when.' She laughed bitterly. 'That might work with those women you go out with, or sleep with, or even,' she added maliciously, 'get engaged to, but as far as I'm concerned you can just take a running jump.'

'Would you have been surprised if I *had* had too much to drink?' Conrad muttered through clenched teeth. 'You'd drive any sane man to drink.'

'And you'd drive any sane woman right into a mental asylum!' Emma yelled.

They looked at each other for what seemed like eternity. In the dim background Emma was aware of the steady ticking of the kitchen clock, the night sounds drifting through the closed windows, the hum of the refrigerator.

She was trembling all over. From the rage or from the heady impact of his body against hers, she wasn't sure. Then, as she opened her mouth to tell him to go to hell, Conrad bent his head and his lips met hers fiercely, crushing all attempts to push him away, under the sheer force of his kiss.

Emma's fists closed uselessly against his chest as she tried not to succumb to the mounting passion firing within her.

His long fingers slid along her shoulders and down her back, and she could feel them with an almost unbearable intensity.

She heard the sound of her own voice telling him to stop, but even to her ears it sounded weak with passion.

His teeth bit gently against the soft skin of her neck, and Emma's head dropped back, like a rag doll.

His hands moved to cup her breasts, and Emma's eyes flew open. If she didn't stop him now, if she didn't stop herself now, then there was no doubt that she would be pulled into her own dizzy need to feel him.

'Let me go,' she said, struggling against an aching want, as she felt his thumbs trace slow circular movements against her nipples. Under her hands, his skin was as hot as hers.

'No!' she said in a high, desperate voice, as his hands slid over her stomach. She pushed him fiercely, and he raised his feverish blue eyes to her.

'Leave me alone,' she said in a strangled tone.

'You want me, Emma.' He moved closer to her, and this time she pushed him away, with as much strength as she could muster. 'Don't retreat behind that wall of ice. You want me, I can feel it. When I touch you, you tremble, and when I kiss you I can feel your longing as strong as I can feel my own.'

There was no use in trying to deny it, and she didn't bother.

'I want you to leave me alone,' she whispered. 'I don't want anything to do with you. You can't give me anything, because you have nothing to give. You use people, and I refuse to be used.'

'What the hell are you talking about?'

'You know as well as I do! Don't think for a moment that I can't see you for what you are! Yes, I might be attracted to you, but that doesn't make me a blind fool!'

God, she thought, if only that were true.

She turned away, walking wordlessly out of the kitchen, and then running up the long staircase, taking the steps two by two, until she reached her bedroom door.

She slammed it behind her, leaning against it, shaking as though she had been through some terrible ordeal from which she had only just managed to escape. With quick movements she stripped off her dress, tossing it into a heap on the floor, and then stepped into the shower. She wanted to bathe away the perspiration covering her. Even under the cold, sharp water her body still burned where he had touched her, each touch erotic and tantalising, promising her the sort of fulfilment which she shamelessly craved.

She found it difficult to sleep that night. She would drift into a light doze, only to find some new image of Conrad leaping out at her when she least expected it. If this was love, then what, she thought with sharp agony, was the point? Every inch of her body seemed filled with pain.

She went over in her mind all the details of the evening, trying to read something behind his actions. All she could see was that he didn't want to give her up. She was valuable to him after all, she thought bitterly, in a very literal sense. She was his passport to Alistair's money.

God, and to think that despite all that, knowing what she did, she was still attracted to him. Not merely attracted, but desperately in love with his humorous, intelligent, caustic charm.

If her feelings hadn't been involved, if she had only been able to treat him as a fling, some kind of temporary aberration, then things would have been so easy. She could walk away and put the whole episode down to experience. Wasn't that how her friends reacted when they broke off from their lovers? They shrugged their shoulders, cried for a few days, and then moved on.

But on, no. Not her. Emma buried her face into the pillow to stifle her sobs. Why had she been stupid enough to fall in love with the man?

She cringed with embarrassment as she remembered how she had responded to his expert lovemaking, opening up to him with total abandon. At least, she thought, she had had the courage to run away from him last night, even though it had been the most difficult thing she had ever had to do.

She had listened to common sense, but she couldn't hide from the fact that every nerve in her body had wanted him then as much as she had wanted him on the boat. As much as she had wanted him from the moment she laid eyes on him.

She had hoped that Sophia would have been a deterrent, that seeing them together would help her to fight the weak-minded craving that threatened to suffocate her. But it hadn't. It had only served to make her more ashamed and confused.

She needed strength, and it was the one thing which he drained from her.

Even in the darkness of the bedroom, the mere thought of his strong brown hands exploring every inch of her was enough to make her tremble with desire.

There was no option left open to her now but to confess everything to Alistair, to tell him about their sham engagement and to try and make him see that she had no alternative but to leave the island on the first flight back to England.

She would return as soon as she had managed to pick up some of the pieces of her wrecked life. After all, they still had their book to finish.

She was pale and tense when she knocked on Alistair's bedroom door the following morning.

It was a cruel twist that he was looking better than she had seen him since he was taken ill. He hustled her into the chair closest to him, prattling on about everything from the weather to his health, fussing around her like a mother hen.

Emma bit her lip anxiously, feeling horribly guilty, and waited for a lull in the conversation before she began speaking.

Bit by slow bit she told him about Conrad's idea, about her agreement, about how much it hurt her to know that they had done the wrong thing.

Alistair listened to her in complete silence, his hands folded on his lap.

'Whose idea was the engagement?' he asked interestedly.

'Conrad's, as a matter of fact.' Emma looked at him in surprise. He had not reacted as she had expected at all. In fact, he had not reacted. He did not seem in the least bit taken aback and she was at a loss to understand it.

'Ah.' Alistair flashed her an avuncular smile.

'Not that it matters,' Emma carried on. 'I agreed, so we're both to blame.'

'Of course,' Alistair soothed. 'It takes two to tango.'

'Aren't you in the least bit disappointed?' Curiosity got the better of her, and she stared at him with open puzzlement.

'These things happen. But why did you decide that now was the time to tell me the truth? Did you think that I had recuperated enough?' He chortled. 'Fancy the pair of you hoodwinking an old man like me. That's not happened to me from as far back as I can remember!'

'We thought that we were doing it for your own good,' Emma rushed in, apologetically. She hoped that he wasn't going to break down. He had taken the revelation so well, but of course it was all a façade.

He was probably going to dissolve into tears any minute now, or else turn away from her in disappointment. Quite possibly both. She looked anxiously at him, waiting for the inevitable.

Instead his sharp eyes returned her stare with equanimity.

'You still haven't answered my question.'

'Question?' Emma asked, bewildered. 'What question?'

'Why did you suddenly decide to tell me about it now?'

'I... Things have changed,' she stammered haltingly.

'Things?'

'Nothing went according to plan.'

'Meaning?'

Emma raised her shoulders helplessly. Why was he asking her this? She had the feeling that she was being kindly but efficiently cross-examined, except for what, she had no idea.

'I... I found out that I couldn't handle the situation.'

It was a flimsy answer, even to her own ears, but she just didn't know what else to say. Alistair had swept aside the whole explanation of their arrangement with a broad-minded wave, and seemed considerably more interested in quizzing her about tiny details which had no bearing on the case at all.

She knew precisely what he would say if she protested. Grandfatherly interest. She had come to realise that he was not without his fair share of tricks which he plucked from up his sleeve without a backward glance. There was no mistaking Conrad's mentor.

'What do you mean, you couldn't handle the situation?'

'Why are you asking me all these questions?' She looked at him with a trace of desperation.

'Grandfatherly interest.'

Emma couldn't hide a smile. 'I knew you'd say that. You're getting predictable in your old age.'

'And you're being evasive.'

'Oh, all right,' she said, giving up, 'I found myself getting too involved with Conrad for my own good.'

'Ah.'

Emma abruptly stood up and went across to the window, staring through it without seeing anything, only aware of feeling thoroughly miserable and horribly vulnerable.

'You've fallen in love with him?'

'More fool me,' she muttered. There was no point in expanding on the subject, and she threw him a look that said that the matter was closed.

'So what are we going to do about the book?' he said with bewildering good humour, changing the subject, much to Emma's relief. 'Not to mention the fact that I'm not going to let you out of my life now that you're here. I've made that stupid mistake once with your mother, and that was once too often. I've been given a second chance with you, and I won't lose you.'

'I'll be back,' Emma responded warmly. 'As soon as I've sorted myself out, I'll be back over. You'll see me before the year's out.'

'Well, you'd better go, then, for the moment. I feel a little tired. And no,' he assured her, reading her expression, 'I'll be quite all right. I just have some thinking to do.'

'Some thinking?' she asked suspiciously.

'Oh, yes, my love. A crossword puzzle I've been working on. I feel I may have solved the last clue.'

'Crossword puzzle? Clue? Grandfather,' she said helplessly, 'sometimes you lose me.'

She turned to leave the room, nodding as he called after her to send Esther up.

It was not yet midday, and already this was proving to be the longest day in her life. The thought of never seeing Conrad again was intolerable. In a way, it was almost better to continue feeling miserable, knowing that he was around, than to return to England and live in a void.

What would she do? The usual routine of theatres and dinners with her friends, some more freelance work although she had nothing lined up, and all the while she would hear the silent sound of the days as they ruthlessly ticked by, reminding her that nothing would ever change.

When she got back to her room, she disconsolately began throwing her clothes into a suitcase, not bothering to think about the horrendous ironing job she would have on her hands when it came to unpacking.

She phoned the airport, only to be told that there were daily flights to Trinidad, but that all connecting flights from Trinidad to Heathrow were fully booked for the next two days.

'Two days!' Emma wailed. 'Is there nothing sooner than that? Like tomorrow?'

'Sorry,' the man automatically said in his businesslike voice. 'Perhaps you would like me to reserve a seat for you for the flight out this coming Thursday?'

'I... Yes, if you could, please.'

She dully gave details of her name, address and telephone number, mentally trying to work out what she was going to do.

Alistair, when she went to see him, had no solutions to the problem. He shook his head ruefully and gave her a brief lecture on the popularity of flights out of the island during the peak season.

He didn't sound in the least bit sorry that she would not be able to leave immediately. There was a distinct glint in his eyes when he told her that they would be able to do some work on the book after all.

'I can't stay indefinitely, Grandfather,' Emma interrupted him gently. 'It's too awkward.'

'Awkward?'

Emma looked at him impatiently. Hadn't she explained it all to him only a few hours before?

'With Conrad.'

'He'll be leaving by the weekend,' Alistair informed her. 'Going back to work. The business can't run without him forever, you know.'

'Of course not.'

Emma digested this bit of information with a sinking feeling. She hadn't given it much thought, but of course

Conrad would be going back to run his companies. Companies didn't just run themselves. They needed someone at the helm. He had already had long enough on the island. Why hadn't she thought about it before? He wouldn't be around, even if she remained here.

Wasn't that just perfect? she told herself, fighting to look pleased with the news.

'Good. I'll cancel my provisional booking and we can get on with the book.'

The phrase 'take up where we left off' sprang to mind, but it seemed so pitifully inadequate that Emma refrained from saying it.

'Good.' Alistair smiled at her in a way that suggested that the conversation was over, and Emma left the room, dawdling on the way back, wondering whether the sun and sea would be so wonderful without Conrad somewhere in the background.

She realised with gloomy resignation that when he wasn't around she felt as though a piece of her was missing.

What a state of affairs for her to have become entangled in. She tried to console herself with the truism that time healed everything. Love would be no exception. In a year's time, she told herself, things mightn't look so bleak, and maybe there would even be someone else around, someone to take Conrad's place.

With a frustrated groan she acknowledged that he had probably spoilt the rest of mankind for her. He had given her something: the bitter-sweet taste of true, burning love. Who could ever provide any kind of replacement for that? One of those well-intentioned colourless men who formed part of her social set? Fat chance!

At least she was doing the right thing in not giving in to him. She told herself to start feeling a little more pleased with herself.

The sight of crumpled clothes, half packed, was just what she couldn't face. She shoved them out of sight on to the chest of drawers and lay down on the bed, covering her face with her hands.

There was a knock on the door, and without bothering to get up Emma mumbled, 'Come in.' Esther, she thought irritably. She didn't want to see anyone, not even kindly Esther. She just wanted to be on her own, to filter everyone else out until those thousands of images of Conrad that filled her mind had been subdued.

She uncovered her eyes, ready to ask Esther if she could come back later on to do the bed, and saw Conrad lounging against the door-frame, looking at her.

He looked alert and watchful, his black hair neatly combed away from his face. He was wearing a pair of faded jeans which emphasised the length of his legs and a pale short-sleeved shirt.

'What do you want?' Emma sprang out of the bed, flushing at the vulnerable position in which he had found her.

Didn't he know that she didn't want to see him? That he was the last person that she wanted to face? Obviously not. You did the right thing, she told herself sternly. He's untrustworthy, never mind how he looks.

'We have to talk.'

'What about?'

Her voice sounded cracked, and she cleared her throat, moving across to the dressing-table and perching on the stool. She would feel more composed the further away she was from the bed.

As though reading the train of her thoughts, Conrad raised one amused eyebrow and proceeded to take her place on the bed.

'About last night, and about what happened on the boat.'

Emma licked her lips which suddenly felt dry.

'We have talked,' she said as casually as she could. 'We talked about it then, and I don't see any point in rehashing the subject. There's nothing more to be said.'

'I think there is.'

'Well, we'll have to agree to differ.'

'Not if I can help it.' He was staring at her in a way that unsettled her. What was it she should remember? Why, she thought frantically, should she be feeling pleased with herself?

She stared back at him, not knowing what to say. A prickle of heat started at her toes and worked its way through her body, until she was burning all over.

'Anyway,' she said stiffly, 'I'd prefer it if you left my bedroom.'

'Why?'

'Because you're invading my privacy,' she said in a tight voice.

'Maybe that's my intention.'

Emma looked at him with alarm. 'That might well be *your* intention,' she said in a colourless, precise voice, 'but it's not mine. I don't want my privacy invaded, least of all by you.'

'Why not? Are you afraid of what you might do, despite all your good intentions?'

'No!'

'Methinks,' he said with wry accuracy, 'the lady doth protest too much.'

'I don't care what you think!'

'Come a bit closer and tell me that.'

Emma remained resolutely where she was. 'Go away. We have nothing to talk about.'

'All right, then, I'll come a bit closer to you. If the mountain won't come to Mahomet, et cetera, et cetera.' He edged himself off the bed, and moved across the room before she had time to take refuge somewhere a little further away.

'Don't try and escape,' he said, reading her mind, and gripping her wrist. Before she could find a suitable retort, he swept her off the stool and carried her struggling to the bed, depositing her ungracefully on it and lying next to her, his arms around her so that she had no room for manoeuvre.

'All right, Mr Strongman. Here I am. You've got me into a position that I can't escape from, and God knows what sort of satisfaction that gives you! If you want to talk, go ahead. Just so long as you leave this room when you're finished, because I don't want to have anything to do with you.'

'You don't mean that.'

'I do!'

'Then why,' he asked with frightening insight, 'are you shivering? If you meant that, you would be lying there as obedient as a mouse and about as responsive.'

Emma stared at him mutinously, hating her body for betraying her.

'Tell me why you don't want anything more to do with me. Answer me that, and I'll leave.'

'Fine!' He wanted to know, then she damn well would tell him. 'You accused me of being a gold-digger,' she said bitterly. 'You had the nerve to insinuate that I was only here for what I could get, when you are hardly an innocent in that area yourself!'

He looked at her with an impatient frown. The man's acting skills, she thought, were beyond compare.

'What the hell are you talking about?'

'Don't try and pretend with me!'

'For God's sake, woman,' he ground out, 'get to the point of this. I haven't got the faintest idea what you're on about. And I'm dying of curiosity.'

'When Sophia called that day to leave that message with you,' she said stiltedly, 'she filled me in on something that hadn't even crossed my mind.'

'Go on.' His voice was soft and menacing, and Emma looked at him warily, wondering whether her confession was such a hot idea. Somewhere at the back of her mind, a vague doubt flitted across. What if Sophia had been wrong? What if Conrad had no interest in Alistair's money? She ignored it.

'Alistair's money,' she muttered grudgingly. 'She told me that it was common knowledge that you stood to inherit Alistair's money...' Her voice wavered, as the puzzled frown gave way to one of derisive comprehension.

He was beginning to follow the gist of what was about to come, and from the looks of it it didn't thrill him.

'Common knowledge with whom?'

'She said...'

'And you believed her.' He looked at her with disgust and stood up.

'Wouldn't you, if you had been in my place?' she asked defensively.

'No. Because I would have used my little grey cells and worked out that any such suggestion was preposterous.'

'It's not preposterous! It makes sense.'

'Oh, yes? Then perhaps you could fill me in on your line of reasoning.'

The nagging doubts about the validity of Sophia's statement were getting stronger, especially when she looked at the thunderous expression on Conrad's face. Anger and scorn blended together, neither of which were doing anything at all for her confidence.

'Why else would you have been so angry at the thought of my being here?' she asked feebly. 'And after you knew about me, why did you make love to me? You were trying to seduce your way into Alistair's money because... because...'

The words died on her lips. Now that she had spoken them, she was overcome with a desire to take them all back.

It was too late for that, of course. The distaste stamped on his face filled her with the growing horror that not only had she been wrong, but also totally off target.

She looked at him bleakly, wishing that the ground would suddenly open and swallow her up. She could cope with his anger, his teasing, his insinuations, but his loathing was unbearable.

'You stupid little bitch,' he said in a cold voice. 'Did it ever occur to you that I was angry at the prospect of your being a gold-digger because I had seen it happen once before to Alistair, and because I love him and feel protective about him? And did it ever occur to you that I made love to you because I wanted you? Not,' he bit out, 'that you can possibly accuse me of seducing you, because the feeling at the time, if I recall, was entirely mutual!'

His words lashed her like invisible whips, hurting her in a way she would not have thought possible.

'Also,' he continued relentlessly, 'if you had used that brain of yours, you might have realised that I don't *need* Alistair's money. I have quite enough of my own!'

'Yes, I guess so, but...' She looked away miserably.

'But nothing! You jumped to all the wrong conclusions because it suited you!' He turned towards the door, glancing around when his hand was on the knob. 'If it's of any interest to you,' he said scathingly from over his shoulder, 'I knew that Alistair had a granddaughter anyway. He told me years ago. I never suspected that the granddaughter was you when you showed up here, but I knew of your existence. I've always known where Alistair's money would go, and I've never given it a thought.'

'Why didn't you say?'

'Believe it or not, I didn't think it was relevant. I didn't think that that narrow little mind of yours would work in that direction anyway.'

'You're hardly pure, driven snow yourself!' Emma said in a high, shaky voice. 'You had no qualms about accusing me of something I wasn't guilty of!'

'Don't try and justify yourself by using that argument.' He looked at her with distaste. 'All I can say is that if you believed that of me, then, lady, I was way off target with you. As far as I'm concerned, you're now in the past tense, and my only regret is that I ever had anything to do with you in the first place!'

He left the room, closing the door quietly behind him, and she could hear the sound of his steps echoing on the wooden floor before he descended the stairs.

Then a dead feeling seeped through her, leaving her too numb to cry, too numb to do anything except stare at the ceiling.

She had misjudged him, and he was right, there was no way she could justify her distrust. She had been an utter fool to have ever listened to what Sophia had told her.

She had believed it because she had wanted to. She had used the knowledge to try and shore up her own defences against him because she had been frightened by the power of her love and by her vulnerability to it.

He didn't love her, and in some weird way she'd thought that she might fight her own love for him by believing the worst of him.

God, how wrong she had been! She still loved him with every ounce of her being, and now not only did he not like her, but his lasting memories of her would be ones of loathing.

She buried her face into the pillow and began to cry.

CHAPTER TEN

EMMA awoke to a feeling of disorientation. The room was in blackness, and she realised that she must have fallen asleep.

She didn't have the energy to get out of bed, even though the clock reminded her that it was nearly seven and only thirty minutes away from dinnertime. She didn't much feel like eating either.

She remained lying where she was, making no effort to fight off the misery gnawing away at her insides.

Conrad detested her. That one thought filled her head and beat away in her mind like the repeated throbbing of a drum. He had left her room with the stamp of disgust on his face, and she had no doubt that she would never lay eyes on him again.

The prospect filled her with anguish, and the anguish glued her to the bed, because all incentive seemed to have left her.

She should be relieved at his decision, she knew that. He might have left, she told herself, believing the worst of her, but at least he had left and she would no longer have to fight the feelings that assailed her every time she looked at him or was in his presence.

Hadn't she convinced herself time and again that her love for him would never be returned? In which case it was much better that he was out of sight, because out of sight might one day be out of mind.

Even if she had not believed a word of what Sophia had told her, even if that disastrous conversation between herself and Conrad had never taken place, things would not have been so dramatically altered.

After all, the fact still remained that she was in love with him, fiercely, passionately and hopelessly in love with him. And he wanted her because he fancied her. The two feelings were poles apart and she had always only been the one who stood to lose.

The truth was, if she was going to be honest with herself, that she would not have been satisfied with lust instead of love, and he had no responsibilities towards her. He was as free as a bird, and any fool knew that birds didn't stay in one place for very long.

He might not have been in love with Sophia, but he had been engaged to her. She, for heaven's sake, had had more of a hold over him.

No, things had worked out for the best. That sour taste in her mouth and the gaping despondency in her soul might try and convince her otherwise, but her head would always protest.

She gazed mournfully at the clock, watching the time tick by, knowing that she should rouse herself and go downstairs, but her body felt like lead, and she could feel her eyelids beginning to droop again.

She reluctantly yielded once more to the panacea of sleep.

She awoke suddenly, with the feeling that someone or something had awakened her.

Her eyes took a while to adjust to the darkness, and then she made out the shadowy form of Conrad, sitting on the bed, looking down at her with an expression which she couldn't quite make out.

She sat up hurriedly, rubbing the sleep out of her eyes.

'You!'

'Yes, me,' he said drily.

'What are you doing here?'

'You brought me back.'

He smiled a slow, wry smile and Emma felt her heart skip a beat, then another as he raised his eyebrows and looked at her ruefully.

'Me?'

'Yes, you. You're a witch, I know that now. You cast a spell over me and I found that, however angry you made me, I couldn't leave.'

She looked at him, her eyes wide and questioning.

'But you had left!' she protested, the lingering smile on his lips bringing a flush of colour to her cheeks. 'When you walked out of this room you told me that you were sorry you ever met me, and that you didn't want anything more to do with me!'

'I guess I made a mistake.'

He stroked her hair, and leaned forward to kiss her on her forehead. Emma sank back with a dizzy feeling against the pillows.

Nothing changed the fact that, whatever he was saying to her now, and however appealingly he said it, he still only wanted her. But as his lips descended to meet her own she closed her eyes and decided just to savour this one kiss. The battle would wait until after that.

She kissed him with restless passion, enjoying his low moanings as he moistened her neck with his mouth.

His hand slipped smoothly underneath her white T-shirt to caress the full soft swell of her breasts.

With a mammoth effort, she pulled away from him, and said in a low voice, 'I can't. You may think me silly and gauche, but I can't make love to you when I know that you don't love me in return.'

Conrad gave a soft, delighted chuckle. 'In return?'

'Well, yes.'

'Are you saying that you love me, Emma Belle?'

She flushed and looked away. What was the point of trying to deny it? She had fallen into her own trap, and maybe it was better that she told him anyway.

'I love you, Conrad,' she muttered under her breath.

'I bed your pardon? I didn't quite catch what you said just then. Something about love...?'

She glared at him, and said in a loud voice, 'I love you! You annoy me, you bewilder me, you make me feel as though I have no control over myself, and I love you for it! Is that loud enough for you?'

'Loud and clear.'

She had thrown all caution to the winds, and she didn't much care any longer. She didn't care if he didn't return her love, it only mattered that he knew how she felt, that she had been honest with him.

She braced herself for the pain that would fill her when he told her that he desired her but that, well, as far as love went, now that was a horse of a different colour.

When he did not say anything, she finally raised her eyes to his. He turned away and switched on the bedside light. All at once the room was suffused in an orange glow, and Emma blinked rapidly.

'I want us to see each other,' he said.

Emma didn't want that at all. The darkness at least provided some shield for her. To have her hurt exposed in the brightness of the room was not what she wanted at all.

She lowered her head, and her hair fell in a gold curtain across her face.

'Look at me,' he murmured, tilting her chin up.

Their eyes met, and he said unhurriedly, 'I love you.'

'What?'

'I love you, Emma. What I do for you is exactly what you do for me, and I adore you for it.'

The blood rushed to her head.

'You're joking!' she whispered incredulously.

Conrad shot her a disapproving glance. 'Now, now, my little witch, why do you insist on believing the worst of me? It's a habit you're going to break out of, you know. It doesn't do my confidence any good at all. Still, we've got a lifetime of trying to cure that particular——'

'What?'

'Don't tell me you didn't hear. I said we've got a lifetime to——'

'Is that a proposal?' she asked tremulously.

'Oh, haven't I said? Will you, Emma Belle, marry me?'

This time the silence was complete. She nodded.

'Yes! Yes, yes, yes!'

'I prayed you might say that.' With a stifled moan, he kissed her face, her eyes, her nose, her mouth.

She felt a wonderful release, as though she had spent the last few weeks balancing precariously on the edge of a cliff, and had now finally found solid ground.

And it felt wonderful.

She sighed with pleasure as he slowly stripped and then proceeded to do the same to her, removing each article of clothing with agonising leisure.

Her body was aching for him, and when they were freed of their clothing she pulled him towards her, delighting in the feel of his naked flesh against hers.

But he was not rushing things. His lips teased her nipples into arousal, and she felt the warmth of his mouth sucking them, nuzzling her breasts, while he stroked her thighs and stomach with his hand.

'I want,' he said huskily, 'to enjoy every inch of you. Making love on the floor of a rocking boat has taught me that I'm too old for that.'

'You seemed to manage all right to me,' she responded languidly.

'Just all right?'

Her laugh was low and throaty. 'Immodest beast. I knew it from the start.'

They made love slowly, as though they had all the time in the world. His mouth caressed the flat planes of her stomach and Emma parted her thighs, drowning in intoxicating need. His tongue delicately circled her navel, and she arched back in pleasure. It was unimaginable that anyone else could arouse her like this. All the men she had been out with were boys in comparison, hollowed-out shells, incapable of exciting her.

When he slid into her, she groaned and moved agitatedly against him.

'God, I've waited for this,' he muttered into her hair.

Emma didn't respond. The waves of pleasure rolling over her had silenced her, had drowned out everything but the delicious fire burning in her.

Was it hours or days later when he lay next to her on the bed, his hand tracing the delicate planes of her face? Emma didn't know. She smiled at him.

'So, Miss Belle, what are you thinking?'

'I'm thinking that another woman might have had all this.' She looked at him from under her lashes, loving the way that his eyes seemed able to darken depending on his mood. They were a deep, drowsy blue now, and she felt her heart quicken.

'Sophia?'

'You were engaged to her! I hate even thinking about it.'

'You have yourself to blame for my breaking off the engagement.'

'You? You little liar!' she teased. 'Sophia told me that she broke it off. Some modelling contract.'

'Well, she simply beat me to it, that's all. Thanks to you, all my well-ordered plans were scattered to the four winds, hard as I tried to hold them together and pretend that nothing had changed. Sophia's modelling contract was a gift from above.'

His hand circled her waist, gently caressing her stomach, moving up to cup a breast.

She rolled to lie on top of him, sighing as his fingers pressed against the length of her spine. Her hair fell, forming a curtain around his face, and she kissed him hard, feeling the rough stubble on his chin where he hadn't yet shaved.

His body moved under her, and he gripped her from behind until they were moving together rhythmically, as one.

For the first time, she understood how people could lock themselves behind closed doors, and spend days in bed. The idea, which she had used to find incomprehensible, now made sense.

She rolled off, holding him against her, feeling his long, lean legs warm against her own.

'Do you know,' he said, 'that I never imagined, when I was waiting for your plane to land, that the woman who got off would turn out to be a stubborn, outspoken she-devil like you who would open up my eyes to something I'd never experienced before?'

'I could be insulted at that description!'

'But you're not.'

'No, because most of those adjectives happen to fit you as well. When I met you, I thought you were the most arrogant, pig-headed person I had ever laid eyes on.'

Conrad threw her a loving glance of mock hurt.

'Now that's really wounding!'

'You're too immodest ever to be wounded!'

'Not true,' he said soberly. 'I would have been more than wounded if I had had to face the prospect of life without you. Just the thought of ever being apart from you makes me sick.'

They looked at each other in silence for a while, then Conrad murmured, 'I can't live without you, my darling.

Do you know that, that night when I came back here looking like something the cat brought in, I'd spent the whole time staring at the sea, trying to work out how I had managed to fall so utterly under your spell. When I got back here to find you and Lloyd like a couple of lovebirds on the sofa...'

His voice hardened, and Emma giggled contentedly.

'We were not like a couple of lovebirds,' she protested. 'We were just chatting about cinema shows and his love-life, of all things.'

'Well, you may not have been cuddling up to him,' Conrad agreed, 'but there was no way that I was going to chance anything happening by vanishing upstairs to bed. Which is what you asked me to do, if I recall.'

'So I gathered. Lloyd was very embarrassed. So far you've been in a foul mood every time you've seen him.'

'You mean the beach?' Conrad said wryly.

'The beach. When I saw you in such an evil temper, I thought that you had had a falling out with Sophia, and then later on she rang and told me that the engagement was off. I guessed that you had taken the news badly.'

'Were you jealous?'

'A bit,' Emma admitted, thinking that that was the understatement of the year.

'You needn't have been. Actually, like everything else since I met you, you were the cause of that.'

Emma looked at him mockingly, feeling his body stir under her.

'Don't play the wide-eyed innocent with me. You can guess why I was in a bad mood.'

'Tell me anyway,' she said lazily, moving closer to him.

'You and that damned Lloyd. That boy has a lot to answer for. When I saw the two of you frolicking together at the beach, I saw red. Never mind about the engagement. That was trifling next to the rage that came over me—he was all over you. I had half a mind to find some excuse to come and drag you forcibly out of the water and bring you back home where I could safely keep my eye on you.'

Emma tried to imagine the scene that would have occurred, and almost wished that he had done just that, although she had no doubt that she would have protested as loudly as she could.

'Why did you ask Sophia to come over here?' Emma asked, suddenly remembering what Sophia had told her at the party.

'Oh, she told you, did she?'

'Not nastily. Just by way of conversation. She said that you insisted that she join you here, and that she came because it was so out of keeping with you.'

'And you put two and two together and came up with five.'

'I thought that you couldn't do without her, if that's what you mean.'

'Precisely what I mean.' He looked at her sideways and she blushed. 'As a matter of fact, I did ask her to come over. To protect me from you.'

Emma stared at him in disbelief. If there was one person in the world who looked less in need of protection, it was Conrad. She could well imagine other people needing protection from him, but not the other way round.

'I was already starting to realise the effect that you had on me,' he continued. 'I thought that it was just my imagination, but just in case I decided to get Sophia over to help put things into perspective. I never believed in love; I certainly never believed that it would hit me like the proverbial thunderbolt. I was wrong.'

'I'd never have guessed,' Emma commented. She remembered thinking how jealous she had been of Sophia. Just seeing them within a foot of each other had been enough to spark off a depth of misery which she had not known herself capable of feeling. If he had not believed in love, then she certainly had likewise thought herself immune to it. When the virus had attacked her, she'd been knocked for six.

'You weren't supposed to,' Conrad remarked drily. 'Falling for you was something I couldn't handle. I could cope with the prospect of an arranged marriage, for all the convenient reasons, but you made me see fast enough that I would have to scrap that idea. Even then, I didn't want to let on to myself what was happening. I kept thinking that I ought to return to work, but somehow I carried on finding reasons to stay.'

Emma watched his dark, striking face and wondered what would have happened if he had called it a day and flown back to London. Would she have recovered? She shuddered at the mere thought of it.

'I did think that your short break for a bit of rest and relaxation was dragging on a bit,' she said pensively.

'So did Gregory Palin at Head Office. I remember him phoning not once but three times, and at last I could use the truthful excuse of telling him that Alistair was ill and I couldn't leave the island until he had recovered. Funny, but I've never suffered from nerves. I could face a hall of stockholders and talk to them without the slightest twinge.'

He looked at her accusingly before continuing, 'From as far back as I can remember, I've made decisions, tackled trade unions, and relished every moment of it. I thought that I was immune to anything remotely resembling uncertainty. I never dreamt that I would meet a woman who could make me a wreck all in a matter of a few weeks.'

He grimaced and Emma laughed softly.

'You might well laugh,' Conrad said drily, 'but I've never had to put myself out for any woman until you waltzed into my life, and then all of a sudden I found myself acting totally out of character. I started being irritated by all kinds of doubts about marrying simply because it was a suitable arrangement, even if Sophia was quite prepared to do the same, and then, even worse, I discovered that I was shying away from the thought of having to leave the island.'

Emma looked at him with amusement, and saw from the flicker of expression on his face that he was still amazed at it.

'I'm glad you stayed,' she whispered, thinking that that was the understatement of her life.

'You didn't give me much choice. You argued with me, gave me sleepless nights, laughed at me. I hope you're satisfied.'

'I couldn't be more satisfied. And, if it's any consolation, you did the same.'

'Good.'

They laughed, and he kissed her gently and lingeringly.

'I only hope that you're not too much of a distraction when we get married.'

'Who, me?' Emma looked at him innocently and grinned. 'This,' she said, 'should ensure that Alistair's back on form in no time at all. I was worried when I told him that the engagement had all been a sham, and that I had fallen in love with you but that it was one way.'

She tried to remember it, but it seemed like a million years away. 'I knew he would have to have found out eventually about us, about the fact that it was all a clever idea on your part to help him recuperate more quickly, but I still hated telling him. I felt like a traitor.'

Conrad shot her an amused glance.

'What's so funny?' Emma asked curiously.

'You are.'

'Me?'

'The situation. What did Alistair say to you when you told him?'

Emma thought back. 'He didn't seem as upset about it as I had thought he was going to be,' she said. 'In fact, he hardly seemed upset at all.'

'The wily old so-and-so.'

Emma looked at Conrad in surprise. 'Why do you say that?'

'Because, my beauty, we weren't the only ones playing the pretend game. Alistair was at it as well.'

Emma propped herself up on her elbow and stared at Conrad, trying to figure out what on earth he was talking about.

'What do you mean, he was at it as well?' she asked, rubbing her ankle against his leg.

Conrad pulled her down to him. 'Don't do that,' he said with a wicked smile.

'What?'

'Slide your foot against my leg. Not when I'm trying to tell you something serious. It throws me off course.'

Emma continued, liking the power of being able to throw Conrad off course. It gave her a satisfying tickle of delight.

'Where was I?' he asked.

'Alistair.'

'Oh, yes. He confessed all to me when I went to see him after I had stormed out of your bedroom. Apparently, he wasn't ill at all.'

'What?' Emma stared at Conrad's face in astonishment.

'The day we rushed back from the party, imagining the worst, it had all been a false alarm, only Alistair decided not to enlighten us.'

'You mean we worried in vain?'

Conrad nodded in amused resignation.

'Alistair was apologetic about the whole thing, but he said that he saw it as a golden opportunity to throw us together. He didn't imagine that we would get engaged, I think he saw that as a bonus from heaven, but he did think that it wouldn't have done any harm if we were united over our concern for him.'

'But what about the doctor?' Emma asked, beginning to see the humorous side of it all.

'Ah. Well, Alistair was ill when he called the doctor out, but it turned out to be only an acute attack of indigestion. Hence his insistence that the doctor not breathe a word to us about his condition.'

It was beginning to slot together. 'But he told us that the doctor said that he didn't know how much longer Alistair had got to live.'

'Poetic licence there. Alistair unconvincingly argued with me that he never told us that he only had a short while left. He said that he told us that the doctor didn't know how much longer, but that it could be decades. Who was to tell? Can anyone predict the length of life given to them? We, he pointed out, merely put the wrong interpretation on his sentence.'

'Well, I never...' Emma settled comfortably against Conrad, feeling the bristle of hair against her breasts.

She was glad that she had worried in vain, and in a way Alistair's ploy had worked. It had thrown them together, even if the method had been a little devious. She would have to have stern words to him about that. Maybe.

She smiled to herself and kissed Conrad's neck, her tongue tracing little patterns on it.

With a low moan, his hand slid around her waist, and he pulled her close to him.

'So all's well that ends well,' he said huskily.

'Are you going to spend the rest of the day talking,' Emma asked wickedly, 'when there's so much more we could be doing?'

'Like what?' Conrad's blue eyes met hers and he raised his eyebrows questioningly.

'You're right. Let's carry on the conversation.'

'We will, you little vixen,' he murmured warmly, 'but later.'

Emma sighed happily. There would be a lot of 'later's from now on.